Praise for

SHOOTING STARS

"Patricia Leavy crafts a riveting narrative that shows the healing power of love and how it helps wounded souls become whole once again."

—*Readers' Favorite*, 5-star review

"For readers seeking a story that restores faith in humanity and shines a light on the beauty of connection, this novel is a must-read."

—*Literary Titan*

". . . there is an alluring hopefulness to the work . . . Beyond the romantic themes, the narrative does manage to tackle several other difficult issues with grace, ranging from grief and self-doubt to self-love and second chances."

—*Kirkus Reviews*

"*Shooting Stars Above* defies category. It grabs hold of your emotions and doesn't let go even after you turn the last page. Leavy's most powerful work to date takes you on a rollercoaster of emotions and leaves you with a brighter sense of the world and the people who quietly make it better."

—U. Melissa Anyiwo, editor of *Gender Warriors*

"Tess's journey and her love for humanity have permeated my very soul. As you turn the last page of this beautifully crafted story, you know the healing process has really just begun. Brava, Patricia Leavy! This story has left an indelible mark on my soul."

—Renita M. Davis, LICSW, PIP, Creatrix,
Illuminated Expressions, LLC

"*Shooting Stars Above* grabbed and shook me in a way most novels do not. The deepest cuts came from Leavy's frankly audacious creation of space for trauma processing and healing as priorities in daily life, rather than the afterthoughts they often become in a world that expects us to smile through pain. It is this sense of empathy for self that haunts me most after reading, and that will likely linger in surprising ways."
—Alexandra Nowakowski, coauthor of
Other People's Oysters

"Leavy's writing is realistic and compassionate. *Shooting Stars Above* is a heartfelt story of love, grief, friendship, and survival that will make you laugh, cry, and most of all feel truly alive. I really loved this book."
—J. E. Sumerau, author of *Transmission*

"*Shooting Stars Above* draws you into its heart and holds you there tightly. Leavy has once again managed to weave her magic through a story that touches on hugely important themes and contemporary issues. Luckily, this is only the first book in a breathtaking series which I have read in full. Each novel is better than the last."
—Alexandra Lasczik, coauthor of
Walking with A/r/tography

"*Shooting Stars Above* is one of the grandest love stories of all time. It celebrates the power and agency of love to hold its own against the darkest forces of hatred and violence. It will make your heart smile."
—Eve Spangler, Associate Professor of Sociology,
Boston College

"While Tess Lee and Jack Miller are healing from past trauma, they learn to love each other in extraordinary ways. This is a wonderful book that you will relish. Read it on your own or in book clubs."
—Jessica Smartt Gullion, author of *October Birds*

"*Shooting Stars Above* will touch readers' lives in important ways. Quite simply, this latest offering from Patricia Leavy is a labor of love. It is well worth reading."
—Keith Berry, coauthor of *Living Sexuality*

"Leavy offers a creative and compelling representation of love and friendship, gender norms and expectations, and the relational nuances of trauma. This novel is another critical contribution to Leavy's extensive oeuvre."
—Tony E. Adams, author of
Narrating the Closet

Praise for
AFTER THE RED CARPET

"Overall, the book is a frothy, sunny read."
—*Kirkus Reviews*

"A fun read from start to finish . . ."
—*Midwest Book Reviews*

"*After the Red Carpet* is a modern masterpiece and a perfect romance narrative from the more literary side of the book world."
—*Readers' Favorite,* 5-star review

"Leavy's writing shines in its ability to delve into the emotional intricacies of a relationship, offering readers a glimpse into the characters' heartfelt explorations of trust, understanding, and mutual support. This novel is an inviting read for those who appreciate a story that reaches the heights of romantic idealism and savors the everyday moments that weave two lives together."
—*Literary Titan,* 5-star review

"Leavy's novels invite you into a world of love and romance like no other. *After the Red Carpet* is a charming, tender, smart, and thought-provoking story about how to maintain personal autonomy after love and marriage. This gorgeous book is so cozy and satisfying, it's like being wrapped in a hug. The ending will make you believe in happily ever after. Highly recommend!"
—Jessie Voigts, PhD, founder of
Wandering Educators

Praise for

THE LOCATION SHOOT

"Each character is more charming than the next . . . the intellectual discussions throughout the book prove fresh and engaging and will keep the pages turning. A quick-witted depiction of moviemaking best suited for contemplative romantics."

—*Kirkus Reviews*

"Patricia Leavy's *The Location Shoot* is hard to put down. . . . Leavy is a master storyteller, skillfully weaving together a narrative that keeps us engaged from start to finish. . . . Ultimately, it's a must-read for anyone looking for a thought-provoking and entertaining exploration of love, relationships, and self-discovery. Highly recommended!"

—*Readers' Favorite*, 5-star review

"The narrative's charm isn't solely defined by the romantic entanglement of a central couple but also by its well-sketched ensemble cast."

—Literary Titan, 5-star review

"A tour de force! Much more than a romance, this novel celebrates the romance of life itself. Leavy's voice in fiction is singular. She brings her laser-like wit, intelligence, and hopefulness to this enchanting and truly unforgettable love story."

—Laurel Richardson, author of *Lone Twin*

Praise for
HOLLYLAND

"This quick read will leave readers satisfied with the happy ending. The main characters will make readers believe in love. Fans of Colleen Hoover and Tessa Bailey will enjoy *Hollyland*."
—*Booklist*

"Some fun secondary characters, a well-drawn setting, and an exciting eleventh-hour kidnapping plot propel Leavy's story."
—*Kirkus Reviews*

". . . Leavy weaves a lot of excitement, charm, and romance into this concise and highly engrossing novel . . . Overall, I would not hesitate to recommend *Hollyland* to fans of romance and women's fiction everywhere; you will not be disappointed."
—*Readers' Favorite*, 5-star review

"Written with the kind of eloquence associated with award winning literary fiction . . . An impressively poignant, laudably original, and thoroughly entertaining novel that moves fluidly between romance, humor, suspense, and joy, *Hollyland* is one of those stories that will linger in the mind and memory long after the book itself has been finished and set back upon the shelf . . . highly recommended."
—*Midwest Book Review*

Shooting
Stars
Above

Shooting Stars Above

A Celestial Bodies Romance

Patricia Leavy

SHE WRITES PRESS

Copyright © 2025 Patricia Leavy

All rights reserved. No part of this publication may be reproduced,
distributed, or transmitted in any form or by any means, including
photocopying, recording, digital scanning, or other electronic or
mechanical methods, without the prior written permission of the
publisher, except in the case of brief quotations embodied in critical
reviews and certain other noncommercial uses permitted by copyright law.
For permission requests, please address She Writes Press.

Published 2025
Printed in the United States of America
Print ISBN: 978-1-64742-854-9
E-ISBN: 978-1-64742-855-6
Library of Congress Control Number: 2024919371

For information, address:
She Writes Press
1569 Solano Ave #546
Berkeley, CA 94707

Interior Design by Tabitha Lahr

She Writes Press is a division of SparkPoint Studio, LLC.

Company and/or product names that are trade names, logos, trademarks,
and/or registered trademarks of third parties are the property of their
respective owners and are used in this book for purposes of identification
and information only under the Fair Use Doctrine.

This is a work of fiction. Names, characters, places, and incidents either
are the product of the author's imagination or are used fictitiously. Any
resemblance to actual persons, living or dead, is entirely coincidental.

NO AI TRAINING: Without in any way limiting the author's [and
publisher's] exclusive rights under copyright, any use of this publication
to "train" generative artificial intelligence (AI) technologies to generate
text is expressly prohibited. The author reserves all rights to license uses
of this work for generative AI training and development of machine
learning language models.

For everyone, everywhere

Chapter 1

"How's your son doing in school?" Tess asked the bartender.

"Really well. He especially loves the history course he's taking."

A man came in and sat two stools down from Tess. They glanced at each other and smiled in acknowledgment.

"Hey, Jack. The usual?"

Jack nodded. "Please."

Tess continued chatting with the bartender as he served Jack a bottle of beer. "The humanities are so important. It's a shame they're undervalued," she remarked.

"You're the expert."

Just then, a different man sidled up to Tess. "You have the most beautiful brown eyes," he said in a smarmy tone.

"Do I?" she asked.

"And the way your hair flows all the way down your back to your slim little waist. You know what they say about dirty blondes?"

"I don't think you should finish that sentence," Tess cautioned.

"I've been watching you. You're a real knockout. Can I buy you a drink?" he asked.

"No, thank you," she replied.

"Come on, just one drink. I'm a nice guy."

"No, thank you," she repeated, turning away.

The "nice guy" opened his mouth to protest, but Jack stood up with an imposing air. "She said no."

The man snorted and walked away.

"Thank you," Tess said, staring straight into Jack's sea-colored eyes.

"Don't mention it. I did feel a little sorry for him, though. You are extremely beautiful, and I can't blame him for taking a shot."

She smiled and pulled out the stool next to her. "My name is Tess Lee. Please, scooch over. Let me buy your drink."

He smiled and took the seat next to her. "Jack Miller. But it's on me. Yours looks nearly empty. What are you having?"

"Sparkling water. I don't drink. It's just a personal choice," she replied.

"Another sparkling water for my new friend," Jack said to the bartender. "So, Tess, what brings you here by yourself?"

"I was supposed to meet my best friend, Omar, but he had a last-minute emergency. His partner, Clay, was pulled over tonight and it became an incident."

"What was he pulled over for?" Jack asked.

"Being Black," Tess replied. "Clay is a surgeon and was on his way home from work. He was pulled over for no reason. The cops ultimately apologized, but he was still shaken up. It's happened to him before. One time he was on his way to an emergency at the hospital, and he was detained even after he showed his hospital ID—appalling. Anyway, I told Omar to stay home with him. They need time together to process and decompress. Omar's Middle Eastern and gets it. I was already in a cab on my way here, so I decided to come anyway. I moved to DC from LA six months ago and don't have that much of a life yet, I suppose. And you?"

"My friends ditched me. We usually get together on Friday nights at a different bar, but they all had to work late. This place is right down the block from my apartment."

"So, what do you do?" she asked.

"I'm a federal agent with the Bureau—counterterrorism. I joined the military right out of high school, Special Forces. I was in the field, often deep undercover, until about a year ago, when I took a desk job as the head of my division."

"Wow, you're like the real-life Jack Bauer. You even look a little like him, with that whole rugged, handsome hero thing you have going on," she said.

He blushed and ran his hand through his light brown hair. "I promise you I'm no Jack Bauer, even on my best day. People thought that character was so tragic, but the real tragedy is that Jack Bauer doesn't exist, and you're stuck with guys like me."

She smiled. "What made you choose that line of work?"

"My parents raised me and my siblings to value community, to be patriotic. My father was in the military and then became a firefighter. The idea of service always seemed important. I wanted to serve my country, to protect people. It's hard to explain, but when I see someone innocent being threatened, I'm willing to do whatever is necessary to protect them. I know it sounds cliché, but I feel like it's my purpose in life."

"That's noble," she remarked.

He shook his head. "The lived reality often isn't. When you spend most of your life in the abyss, it gets pretty dark."

"A residue remains, right?" she asked.

He looked at her intently, a little surprised. "Yes, exactly."

"I understand. You convince yourself it's all been for something that matters more than you do, that whatever part of yourself you sacrificed was worth it, because it simply has to be."

He looked at her as if she had read his innermost thoughts. "Yes," he said softly. "Tell me, what do you do?"

"I'm a novelist."

"What are your books about?"

"That's a difficult question to answer. I guess I wanted to write about everything: what it means to live a life, why it's so hard, and how it could be easier. To walk people through the darkness, in a way. Perhaps my goals were too lofty, and in that respect, each book fails more spectacularly than the one before."

The bartender smirked.

Tess wistfully said, "Maybe reality can never live up to our dreams."

They continued talking, completely engrossed with one another. Two hours later, Jack said, "I live nearby. Do you want to come over for a cup of coffee?"

Tess looked him straight in his warm eyes. "I'd love to."

He threw some money down on the bar to cover both tabs. The bartender said, "Ms. Lee, are you sure you're all right? I can call you a cab."

"You're very kind, but I'm fine. Thank you."

Jack opened the door and held it for Tess. "Do you know the bartender?"

"Just met him tonight," she replied.

"Down this way," Jack said, taking her hand as if it were completely natural. They approached a homeless man on the corner asking for money. Tess walked right up to him, pulled a twenty-dollar bill from her pocket, and handed it to him. She held his hand as she passed the bill, looked in his sunken eyes, and said, "Be well."

As they walked away, Jack said, "That was really sweet, but you should be more careful."

"I trust my instincts," she replied.

When they arrived at Jack's small apartment, he took her coat. She glanced around and noticed the walls were completely bare. "How long have you lived here?" she asked.

"About nine years," he replied. "Can I get you some coffee or something else to drink?"

She shook her head slowly and meandered over to his bedroom. He followed and they stood face-to-face, looking deeply into each other's eyes. He took the back of her head in his hand and started to kiss her, gently and then with increasing passion. She slipped her hands under the hem of his shirt and pulled it off, and they continued kissing. As he leaned back to admire her, she noticed the scars on his muscular body: two on his right shoulder, another on his abdomen, and smaller marks along his upper arms. When he noticed her looking, he turned around to lower the light, revealing the gashes across his back. She lightly brushed her fingers along the deep marks.

"I'm sorry," he said, turning to face her. "War wounds. A couple of gunshots. Some other stuff from when I was in the Gulf and later doing undercover work. I know it's gruesome."

"It's wonderful," she whispered.

"What?" he said.

"I'm sorry, I didn't mean it that way. It's just that I've never seen anyone whose outsides match my insides."

He looked at her sympathetically.

"I was abused when I was little. My grandfather and my uncle. It started when I was eight. No one can see my wounds, but they're there."

He stood still, looking into her doe eyes as if time had stopped and she were the only person in the world.

"I'm so sorry. I've never shared that with any man I've been with in my entire life, and I just met you. That has to be the least sexy thing ever. I'll leave," she stammered, trying to move past him.

He took her hand and pulled her back toward him. They stared into each other's eyes, piercing straight through layers of pain, to the pure soul hidden away, waiting to be discovered. He cupped her delicate heart-shaped face in his hands, gently caressed her cheeks, and leaned forward, resting his forehead against hers. They stood with their foreheads pressed together for a long intimate moment, just breathing. Jack drew back and lightly brushed his lips against hers. She reciprocated and they began kissing again. He slowly untucked her shirt and pulled it over her head as her hair fell in cascades, and then he unhooked her lace bra in one motion. He kissed her mouth, ear, and neck before moving down to her breasts, gently licking her pale pink nipples. She unbuttoned her jeans and he helped her shimmy out of them, slowly peeling off her underwear before removing the rest of his clothes. They ran their hands over each other's bodies, climbed into bed, and made love with their eyes locked, no words spoken.

Afterward, he held her in his arms, and they exchanged tender kisses. "That was so special," he whispered. "I know it's crazy to say this, but I've never felt this kind of connection before."

"Me either," she whispered in return.

"Spend the day with me tomorrow."

"Okay," she replied, and they fell asleep, their limbs entangled.

The next morning, Tess awoke to find a note on the pillow beside her that read, *Went to get breakfast. There's an extra toothbrush on the bathroom counter. Back soon.*

She rummaged around in one of his drawers and pulled out a long-sleeved white shirt. She slipped it on and brushed her teeth, and by the time she was done, Jack had returned.

"Hey, sweetheart," he said, as if they had known each other for years. He pecked her on the cheek and rubbed her shoulder. "You look sexy in this."

"I hope you don't mind . . ." she started.

He pressed his mouth to hers. "Of course not. I like seeing you in my clothes." She smiled and he continued, "I didn't know what you like, so I got bagels, muffins, and a fruit salad. Do you want coffee?"

"Yes, please. Black."

He poured two mugs of coffee, and they sat down at the small table. "What kind of food *do* you like?" he asked.

"For breakfast, I usually have a little oatmeal, sometimes eggs. I'm a vegetarian. I don't believe in hurting living beings."

Jack looked down, a hint of shame on his face.

"Innocent beings," she added.

He smiled. "I guess that's why you're so tiny."

She started picking at the fruit salad. Jack watched her moving it around with her fork, almost like she was counting. He looked at her quizzically.

"I'm weird with food. I don't eat that much and sort of monitor every bite. It's kind of a control thing. It's a lot worse when I'm struggling with something in my life." She paused, keeping her eyes on her breakfast. "I have problems."

He reached across the table and put his hand on hers. "That's okay. We all have problems. They make us human."

Tess smiled faintly and they gazed at each other, with a look of true understanding and acceptance.

After breakfast they made love and then lay in bed silently for an hour, running their hands along each other's arms. Jack kissed the beauty mark on her shoulder. Tess skimmed her fingers across the scars on his arms and whispered, "I know you've experienced unimaginable pain . . . that you've seen the worst of humanity."

He ran his fingers down her cheek. "I know you have too."

"Maybe it's why our connection is so inexplicably strong. Maybe we're each other's candle in the dark cave."

"Maybe we're each other's way out of the cave," he said, and planted a tiny kiss on the tip of her nose.

"Jack, I feel so incredible being like this with you."

"Me too. I could stay like this forever."

"I know it doesn't make sense, but I feel so close to you, so safe with you," she said.

"Me too."

They leaned forehead to forehead. She pulled back and sprinkled little kisses on his bicep.

He placed another tiny kiss on the tip of her nose and whispered, "As hard as it is to tear ourselves out of bed, maybe we should take a shower and figure out what to do today."

"Okay."

"What do you feel like doing? I'll take you absolutely anywhere you want to go."

"How about we just take a stroll around your neighborhood. Then maybe we could find a game or a movie on TV. I don't need anything fancy. Let's just spend time together."

He kissed her forehead and said, "That sounds perfect."

Later that evening, they enjoyed Chinese takeout straight out of the containers. "This veggie lo mein is delicious," Tess remarked as she slurped down the long noodles. She clasped another bite with her chopsticks and held it in front of Jack. "Here, try some."

"That's so good," he agreed when he finished chewing. "You're an expert with those chopsticks."

"I've traveled to Asia quite a bit. You know, Jack, you didn't have to make the whole order vegetarian. I want you to have whatever you want. I believe in accepting people as they are. I would never try to change you," Tess said as she skillfully maneuvered a dumpling out of its container.

"That's sweet. I believe in accepting people too. I confess to being a carnivore, but I'm happy to eat this way for a change. I'm easy."

She smiled and looked around. "Why is your apartment so empty? You've been here for years, and there's nothing on the walls other than this beige paint—which I'm guessing was here when you moved in."

"This place has always been a crash pad more than a home. Work has been my life for a long time. Especially when I was out in the field, on undercover operations. Sometimes I wouldn't be here for months at a time. I took a desk job so I'd have a shot at a personal life. I've never really had much of a life of my own. Until maybe now." He smiled, paused, and added, "Besides, I'm a pretty simple guy. I don't need much."

Tess smiled and grabbed the container of tofu in garlic sauce. "This is delicious," she remarked, and she joyfully took another big, uninhibited bite.

After dinner they made love once more and fell asleep in each other's arms.

Sunday morning, Tess realized she'd missed a dozen calls and text messages from Omar. She called him while Jack was making coffee.

"I promise, I'm fine. I'm sorry I worried you. I met someone. His name is Jack. He's special . . . Well, if he *is* holding me hostage, don't pay the ransom. I want to stay . . . I'll text you all about it . . . Okay, love you too. Bye."

"He was worried about you?" Jack asked.

"He's been looking out for me for a long time. We talk every day, but I guess I was too preoccupied yesterday," she said, slipping her hands around his waist.

"Sounds like a good friend," Jack remarked.

"He's more than that; he's my family. He moved here a year ago and convinced me to leave LA so we could be in the same city. But enough about him. Right now, I'm only interested in you. Come here," she said suggestively, walking backward toward his bedroom and motioning with her finger. Just as he was about to touch her, she grabbed a pillow and walloped him.

"Oh, you're in trouble now," he teased, darting for a pillow. They tumbled onto the bed, laughing.

They spent the rest of the day lounging around Jack's apartment, reading the Sunday newspaper, and sharing stories. That night before they went to sleep, Jack brushed the hair from Tess's face and said, "I don't want the weekend to end. Do you have to work tomorrow?"

"Well, I do work for myself. Can you take the day off?"

"I once took two weeks off, but other than that, I've never taken a single day off in over twenty years. So yeah, I think I'm due for a personal day."

The next day, Tess and Jack went for a walk and ended up at a local park, fallen leaves scattered on the ground. They sat on a bench, huddled together in the late autumn chill.

"I love this time of year," Tess remarked. "Most people prefer the gorgeous, colorful leaves, but I've always liked it when they fall, and the trees start to become bare."

He looked at her adoringly. "Tell me why."

"I've never seen it as death, but rather as a shedding of the past." He rubbed her arm and she continued, "Most people wait for the trees to bloom again before they admire them. But I think they're at their most beautiful when they're bare. Stark, simple, alive . . . shy in a way. It's like there's an honesty, a vulnerability. There's awe-inspiring strength too. They're persevering, surviving, waiting patiently for the bounty that will come sure as the sun will rise, as if they innately trust that the bitter cold darkness will pass. It's so beautiful when strength and vulnerability coexist."

"The way you look at things is so special. It's already changing how I see. Must come from being a writer."

She smiled.

"Tell me more about your writing," he said.

"In a way I create story worlds so I can crawl into them, hide, put my feelings someplace. Sometimes those worlds aren't so happy. They can be filled with despair and suffering. But I find as I trudge through them, I get to another place, and the characters do too." She shrugged. "Perhaps readers do too. At least I hope so."

He leaned forward and gently pressed his lips to hers. "The way you explain your work is beautiful. I'm not good with words."

"Yes, you are," she said. "Some people use words sparingly because they know that's all they need. I admire that. There's honor to it, and honesty, like the strong bare trees." He ran his finger down her cheek, and she added, "Besides, sometimes words aren't necessary at all." She pecked his lips and they smiled at each other. Suddenly, a little boy in a red jacket ran over and tugged at Tess's coat sleeve.

"Do you have superpowers?" he asked. "My dad says you do."

"Excuse me?" she replied.

His father came running over, looking embarrassed. "I'm so sorry if he was bothering you, Ms. Lee."

"Not at all," she replied with a gracious smile.

"I'm a librarian. I want to thank you for everything you've done," he said.

"My pleasure," she replied. "Thank you for what *you* do."

The little boy tugged at her sleeve again. "Well? Do you have superpowers?"

His father laughed. Tess looked at the boy and lowered her voice conspiratorially. "I'll tell you a secret. Everyone has superpowers, they just don't know it."

"Even me?" he asked.

"Especially you," she replied.

Jack smiled.

The man took his son's hand. "I think we've bothered these people enough. Thank you again, Ms. Lee," he said, leading his son down the path.

Jack looked at Tess. "That was so sweet, what you said to that boy."

She leaned over and gave him a little smooch.

"What was the deal with his father? It seemed like he knew you."

"I did some volunteer work for the library a few months ago. It's something I do from time to time," she explained.

A few little girls came skipping past them, drawing their attention. Jack suddenly seemed far away. After a moment passed, Tess touched his hand, pulling his gaze back to her.

"It's starting to get cold. You want to go to a movie?" he asked.

"Sure."

After the movie, they stumbled into a neighborhood Italian restaurant for dinner. The maître d' greeted Tess like an old friend. "Ms. Lee, such a pleasure. We have our best table for you."

"I guess you've been here before," Jack said as he pulled out her chair.

Soon, Tess was scraping the last bite off her plate. "How were the meatballs and spaghetti?" she asked.

"Awesome," Jack replied, taking a piece of bread and sopping up the marinara sauce on his plate. He popped it in his mouth. "That was so good. Tasted completely homemade."

"I'm guessing you don't get a lot of home-cooked meals."

He shook his head. "Mostly takeout, prepared meals, that kind of thing. We had big family dinners every night when I was growing up. It seems like another lifetime now." He sighed. "The career path I took didn't allow room for family. I've been on my own a long time."

"Has that been difficult?" she asked.

"I made peace with it. Doing my job required blocking everything else out. Focusing on the task at hand."

"I understand. I try to be fully present in the moment. To forge ahead and not get weighed down by the past. It allows me to do what needs to be done, sharing the deepest parts of myself in my novels and everything else required of me as an author. We share this, you and I, the ability to block everything out to focus on what's right there."

"I know. I could see it in your eyes from the first night we met."

She reached across the table and put her hand on his. "Jack, listen to the music."

"Sinatra—the best."

"Let's dance," she said.

He looked around. "I don't think they have dancing here."

"But I love to dance. Let's live in the moment."

He stood up and took her hands, and they danced by the table. "You know, I'm not much of a dancer, but I promise to dance to as many slow songs as you want."

"Maybe someday we'll have a special song," she said, nuzzling into his chest.

Later, when they got back to Jack's apartment, he led her to the couch with a slightly serious look. "I need to tell you something."

"What is it?" she asked.

He took her hands and looked into her eyes. "You've seen the scars on my body, but there's another side of it. When you talk about living in the moment to do what needs to be done, I understand all too well. For many years, much of my work happened behind closed doors, racing the clock to prevent imminent threats. I had to do whatever was necessary to get the intel we needed. By any means. That's in the past now, but Tess, I've done things—things that may be unimaginable to someone as sweet as you, things I had to do to protect innocent people." He proceeded to tell her every act of violence he had ever committed, his life laid bare at her feet. The list was long, the death count high.

When he finished, she said, "You did what you had to do for your job. I don't understand why you're telling me this."

"Because I'm in love with you. I'm completely, madly in love with you, and I've never felt that way about anyone. It's important to me that you know I've struggled with what's been required of me. It was necessary, but it wasn't easy or how I wish the world were. I didn't know if I could ever share this with someone. It's why I accepted being alone. But God, I'm in love with you, Tess. With the things I've done, I don't expect that you could ever feel that way about me, but I needed you to know who I am." He looked down.

She stroked his cheek. "Jack, I'm in love with you too. I spent our first night together memorizing your face: every line, edge, ridge, pore. I knew you were the best thing that would ever happen to me, and I was afraid the memory would have to last a lifetime."

He kissed her, skimming her cheek with his fingertips. "Baby, you've made me so happy. I feel like the luckiest man in the world."

"Jack, let's not worry about all of the details of our pasts. I want to leave the pain behind and just love each other now."

"Okay, but maybe I should at least know how old you are and when your birthday is."

"Thirty-eight, and I never cared for holidays, including birthdays."

"Got it. Forty-two, and sweetheart, you're the only present I'll ever need."

She smiled.

"Tess, I see who you are like I can see inside of you. I see your kind, gentle heart, your strength, and your vulnerability. I see you." Her eyes became misty. He used his thumbs to wipe the wetness and continued, "I know how you make me feel, and I love you. There's nothing else I need to know."

"I feel the same way about you."

"When we look into each other's eyes, it's so intense, so truthful. Somehow, we see each other. I needed to be honest with you, to protect what we have. Protecting this thing between us means everything to me. Now we can leave the past behind us."

She smiled. "My entire adult life, I've tried to live only in the moment. I'm able to do that easily with you."

He ran his finger along her hairline and whispered, "Let's go to bed."

The next morning, Jack went to work and Tess went home. At the end of the day, they met at his apartment. "I have something for you," he said, holding out a black velvet box. "I was passing an antique store and saw it in the window."

She opened the box to reveal a gold heart locket. She beamed and her eyes filled with tears. "Jack, it's the best present I've ever received," she said, putting it around her neck. "I'll wear it every day."

"You have my heart, Tess. My whole heart, forever."

"Promise me something. Don't ever buy me another present again. Nothing could ever be better than this."

"I'm hoping life is long. That's a lot of birthdays, holidays . . . Tuesdays," he said.

"Flowers. You can always get me flowers if you want to," she replied.

"Which ones are your favorite?"

"White hydrangeas. I never buy them for myself," she said.

They kissed, and then Jack got up and turned some music on. He reached for her hand. "Let's dance."

The second song that played was "All of Me" by John Legend. Two lines into the song, Jack said, "This is our song, I just know it is. Okay, baby?"

She nodded and rested her head on his firm chest.

They continued to work each day and spend each night together. Thursday night, Tess made grilled eggplant parmesan, which she brought over to share with Jack. While they were eating, he said, "My friends and I go to this place called Shelby's Bar every Friday night. I told them all about you, and they really want to meet you. Will you meet us there?"

"Of course," she replied. "Tell me about them."

"Joe is in his mid-fifties. We've worked together for about fifteen years, although he's always had a desk job and was never in the field. He's a class act. Bobby is young, twenty-nine, and the nicest, most laid-back guy. He joined the Bureau three years ago, but I feel like I've known him forever. His girlfriend, Gina, is an elementary school art teacher. You'll like her."

"Sounds great. What do you think about bringing an overnight bag and staying the night at my place after we hang out with your friends? It's about time you see it. Omar and Clay are coming over for brunch on Saturday, and I'm dying for you to meet each other. Will you?"

"Absolutely," he replied.

"Do you think it will seem strange to our friends, how deeply we feel about each other after such a short time?" she asked.

"I don't know. But no one can ever truly understand the depth of the darkness we've both survived, what we see in each other, and why we just want to love with our whole hearts. I can hardly explain it to myself. How could anyone else ever get it?"

"Jack, you know how people always talk about all the things they want to do or see in their lifetime? They don't even mention being happy because I suppose they think that's just a given."

"Yeah."

"Happiness has never been a given for me. I guess I pursued other things," she said.

"Me too," he replied.

"But I'm so happy now, with you."

"I love you so much, Tess."

"I love you too."

Chapter 2

"Joe, I'm completely in love with her," Jack said, taking a swig from his beer.

"You've always been such a loner. I honestly never thought I'd see the day," Joe replied.

"I told her how I felt, and it didn't scare her. She said she loves me too, and I know she means it."

"I can't wait to meet her."

"She's sweet, smart, and so beautiful. There's a gentleness about her, this deep kindness in her eyes. From the first night we met, there was something indescribable between us. No one has ever gotten to me like this. It's like my heart just cracked wide open," Jack said. He took a sip of his beer. "All I want to do is spend time with her."

"You deserve happiness, something for yourself. Long overdue. I'm thrilled for you," Joe said.

"She'll like this place, especially when the music comes on later. She loves to dance."

Joe's mouth fell open. "You dance?" he asked in disbelief.

"The slow songs, as many as she wants."

"Wow, you've fallen hard."

Jack smiled. "There she is," he said when Tess walked through the door, dressed casually in jeans and a fitted black sweater.

They both stood up as she approached the table.

"Hi, sweetheart," Jack said, kissing her. "This is my friend Joe. Joe, this is—"

"Tess Lee," he interrupted, staring in awe. "It's a real honor to meet you."

Jack looked at him curiously.

"Nice to meet you too," she replied.

"I didn't realize . . . Jack never mentioned," Joe stuttered, running his hand through his salt-and-pepper hair. "Well, he never said your last name. Uh, please, let's sit."

They all sat down, Jack and Tess in the booth, and Joe in one of the surrounding chairs.

"This place is cool," Tess observed, looking around the casual room that featured cheap gray flooring, a bar with a flat-screen television, tables topped with bowls of pretzels, and a small dance floor. "Is this for me?"

"Yes, I ordered you a sparkling water," Jack replied.

"Thank you," she said, taking a sip.

"Tess, this is truly an honor. Your writing is wonderful. I've read many of your books," Joe gushed.

"You're very kind," Tess replied.

Bobby was the next to arrive. He dropped into a chair next to Jack, extended his hand, and said, "You must be Tess. Great to meet you." Then he signaled for the waitress to bring him a beer. "Gina should be here any minute. She had parent-teacher conferences this week." He grabbed a fistful of pretzels and started munching on them. "You look really familiar," he said to Tess. "You must have one of those faces."

Tess smiled.

Bobby continued, "Everyone needs to be extra nice to Gina tonight. Yesterday this one jerk said he wished his kids spent more time in math and less in her art class. You can imagine how she felt. God only knows what happened in those meetings today. Tess, you must relate. Jack said you're a writer."

Tess's smile grew.

"Bobby," Joe said softly. "Actually, Tess is—"

But before he could finish, Gina flitted over. Bobby stood up and gave her a peck. "Hey, babe. I just got here a minute ago. This is Tess."

Gina's jaw dropped. She patted Bobby on the chest as she fell into her chair. "Bobby, this is Tess Lee. *Tess Lee!*"

Jack looked at Tess, a little lost, as he was with Joe's reaction to her.

"I'm sorry," Gina said, staring straight at Tess with eyes like saucers. "I'm just in shock. I love your work so much. This is just incredible."

"Well, it's very nice to meet you, Gina. You're very kind," Tess replied.

Gina turned to Bobby. "Is this really happening?"

Tess looked down and put her hand on Jack's leg. Her cell phone rang, so she retrieved it from her handbag and looked at the screen to see who was calling. "I'm so sorry, I don't mean to be rude, but this is an international call I've been missing all week. Please excuse me while I step outside for a minute."

As soon as Tess was out the front door, Gina hit Bobby's arm. "Why didn't you tell me? She must think I'm a moron, the way I was blabbering like a demented fangirl."

"What are you talking about?" he asked, pretzels spilling from his hand.

"What's going on?" Jack asked, furrowing his brow.

"Jack, Tess is one of the most successful authors in the world," Joe said.

"And my personal hero," Gina added. She turned to her boyfriend. "Bobby, her books are on my nightstand.

You've seen her picture a thousand times. Not to mention she's been interviewed on all the late night and morning talk shows."

Bobby shrugged.

"You really don't know who she is?" Joe asked Jack.

"I guess I don't read a lot," he replied.

"They make movies and limited series out of her books too. You probably know who she is, but you just don't realize it," Joe said.

Bobby picked up another handful of pretzels. "Gee, Jack. I would've figured you'd have done a full background check on any girl you brought home. You didn't even google her?"

Jack looked to Joe, who blurted out, "She's worth over five hundred million dollars, Jack."

"I had no idea," he mumbled, shaking his head.

"It's a remarkable story," Joe continued. "She published her first novel right out of college. It was a start-up publishing house, and they accepted unsolicited submissions. She didn't even have an agent. Her book became an international bestseller and won a slew of awards."

"Yeah, readers had super emotional responses to the book and a bunch of influencers spread the word, reviewers caught on, and it completely took off," Gina interjected.

"The next book hadn't been contracted to anyone yet, so publishers had a bidding war trying to get their hands on it." Joe puffed and continued, "She had so much power and used it in the cleverest way. Instead of taking a seven-figure advance from one of the big publishers, she agreed to stay with her small indie publisher under special conditions. Bottom line, they would distribute the English-language version of her books, but she retained all the rights: copyright, licensing, translations, entertainment, the works. It was an unprecedented deal that allowed her to build an empire. She releases a novel every year and has a famous collection of essays. To this day, she doesn't work with an agent, so she's never had to give a cut to anyone and she controls how her work is adapted and distributed around the world."

"How do you know all of this?" Jack asked in astonishment.

"I read about it in *Time* magazine and *Newsweek*. She was the cover story."

"She's been on the covers of all the fashion magazines too, because she's so gorgeous on top of being super famous and talented. She gives most of what she earns to charity," Gina added.

"We were in the park the other day, and this man thanked her for something she had done for a library," Jack said. He paused and shook his head. "She said she had done some volunteer work."

"She's donated millions to public libraries and raised tens of millions more. I read that she's had a grueling book tour schedule for most of her career, and that while she's on the road, she gives public talks promoting literacy and advocating for the arts," Joe said.

Gina picked up Bobby's beer and guzzled it. "Wowza. Okay, I can breathe now. Yeah, Joe's right. Every librarian, humanities teacher, art teacher, and aspiring writer I know idolizes her, not to mention women in the business world. She's a legend."

Jack sat for a moment, trying to process everything. He noticed Tess come through the front door. "Excuse me," he told his friends, getting up and crossing the bar to meet her.

"I'm sorry," she said. "I hope your friends don't think I'm rude. I've turned that stupid phone off for the rest of the night."

He put his hands on her shoulders, barely able to look at her. "I'm so embarrassed."

"Why? What happened?" she asked.

He looked down, as if searching for the words. "I didn't know who you are," he muttered.

"I don't understand. You know me better than anyone."

"But . . ." He trailed off, glancing back toward their table.

"Ah. That isn't who I am, it's what I do. Sometimes it confuses people." Her expression took on a glint of sadness. "You're not confused, are you?"

He looked into her eyes and brushed the hair out of her face. "No, baby, I'm not confused."

"I love these old brownstones. Which floor are you on?" Jack asked as they walked up the front steps.

"The whole thing is mine. It was converted into one giant home years ago. I was lucky to snag it when I moved to DC," Tess said as she unlocked the door. "Come on in." They entered the large open-concept kitchen and living room with dark wood floors, light gray walls, and crown moldings. She dropped her handbag on the long marble island. "Let me take your jacket." He handed her his jacket, which she hung in an organized closet.

Jack gazed around as Tess said, "Your friends are great. They're so much fun."

"They loved you too. I think you made Gina so comfortable by the end of the night that she actually started to see you as a real person."

Tess giggled. "Your friends were really talking you up too. They think the world of you. Do you know how many times they told me you're the most honorable, loyal person they know?"

"I guess they thought I needed help," he joked.

"Well, you don't," she said, wrapping her arms around him.

They looked into each other's eyes, and then Tess's gaze dropped. Jack touched her chin and gently raised her gaze to meet his. "What is it, sweetheart?"

"Jack, in the bar we didn't really get to talk about what your friends told you, that I'm, well, people know me, or Tess Lee. That's not the name I was given. I chose it for myself. I changed my name when I left home. To me, Tess Lee is someone I created. She's the author. I'm just Tess." She took a breath, and he waited patiently until she continued. "I never wanted any kind of attention or spotlight, only to be a writer. My story worlds, the characters, they're my salvation. It's very personal. Fame is the last thing I wanted. It's a sacrifice I've learned to live with to share my work, try to make people feel less alone, and give back as much as possible." He ran his finger along her hairline, and she added, "I think you can stop fame from changing you more easily than you can stop it from changing everyone else. There's a certain allure, a fascination that influences how people see you, forever. I would be heartbroken if that ever happened with you . . ."

"Shh," he whispered. He cupped her face in his hands and gently kissed her forehead. "Tess, I've seen exactly who you are since our first night together, and nothing will ever change that. You're my Tess and I'm your Jack. Like I promised, you have my whole heart. Forever." She smiled brightly. He caressed her shoulders and then craned his neck to look around. "This place is gorgeous."

"It's too big for me, but that's what I get for buying it sight unseen. Omar picked it out. The dining room is around the corner, my bedroom is down that way, the second floor has guest rooms, laundry, and a gym, and the top floor has been converted into an obscenely massive library and office. You can poke around tomorrow."

"I don't know much about art, but these paintings are great. Modern."

"They're all by unknowns. Some were bought in the street. I like to support living artists."

"It looks like you've lived here for years," he remarked, admiring the keepsakes scattered around. "Hard to believe it's only been months."

"When Omar convinced me to move here, he promised to have the house set up so it would feel lived in and I wouldn't lose writing time. He's a man of his word."

"But what about the mantel?" Jack asked. "It's empty. It would be a nice spot for photos."

"I don't really have any photos," she said.

"Hey," he said. He pulled her closer to him and wrapped his arms around her waist. "Show me your bedroom."

When Jack woke up the next morning, Tess was already showered and ready for the day. She was slipping a bracelet on when she noticed he was awake. She sat down beside him on the bed and gave him a kiss. "Good morning, baby."

"Good morning, sweetheart," he said. "I slept like a log. What time is it?"

"After nine. You were tired. I'm glad you're comfortable here. Omar and Clay will be here at noon. I need to run to the bakery to pick up the desserts I ordered, and then I'll get the frittata ready. I'm making artichokes because Clay is mad for them."

He scooched over and lifted the blanket. "Come spend a few minutes with me first. I'll go to the bakery, so you have time."

She crinkled her face. "Well, I guess if you'll do that, we can be cozy for a few minutes."

She crawled into bed and leaned against him.

"Tell me about Omar and Clay. You made a hell of a

first impression on my friends; now I need to do my part with yours."

"They'll love you because I love you. Omar is my everything—well, until you. He's my best friend and my only family. We've been a team since college. We adore each other, rely on each other. I couldn't survive without him."

"Where's he from? What does he do?"

"He was raised in London, went to college in New York with me, and then moved to Chicago for graduate school. He's a clinical psychologist, but by the time he graduated, I desperately needed someone smart whom I could trust to run my licensing business, and he's such a good friend that he agreed to help me out. He changed his whole life for me. Who does that? I don't know how I got so lucky."

"That's incredible," Jack said.

"He still does his own work part-time. He moved here about a year ago when he got a big research grant from the National Institutes of Health. He's part of a team that is studying how art impacts our emotional intelligence and well-being. It's amazing work."

"Sounds like an impressive guy."

She nodded. "He's super smart but not at all uptight. Quite the opposite. He's sarcastic and wickedly funny. His favorite sport is mockery. Loves teasing me in his posh British accent. Of course, I can hold my own."

"No doubt," he said with a chuckle. "And Clay?"

"They've been together about four years, and I absolutely adore him too. He's a trauma surgeon and the nicest man you could ever meet. A class act. He's been very generous. For years my life was an endless string of book tours and everything that comes with that. Omar traveled with me when he could and spent loads of time at my place in LA. Clay has always respected our relationship. It's easier now that we're all in the same city. It's why I agreed to move here. Omar had done so much for me, and I felt it was my turn. You'll love them."

"Well, I'd better hop in the shower because I don't think we want them to find us like this."

Tess giggled. "I'll go make coffee."

✦ ✦ ✦

Omar and Clay arrived at noon.

"Hello, Butterfly," Omar said, kissing the top of her head.

"These are for you," Clay added, handing her a large bouquet of pink flowers.

"They're beautiful, thank you. This is Jack," she said, touching his chest. "And this is Omar and his better half, Clay."

Omar shot her the side-eye.

"Nice to meet you," they all said, shaking hands.

"Let me take your jackets. Brunch is in the living room, please go sit," Tess said.

Jack sat on the couch, and Omar and Clay took the chairs. "What can I get everyone to drink?" Tess asked.

"Well, it's brunch, Butterfly. There bloody well had better be cocktails," Omar joked.

"Of course. What would you like? A mimosa?"

Omar nodded.

"Make it two, please," Clay said.

"When in Rome," Jack added.

Tess went to retrieve the drinks while the men chatted.

"Tess has told me a lot about you guys," Jack said.

"Likewise," Omar replied. "In the twenty years I've known her, she's hardly shown any interest in the many would-be suitors who have tried to catch her eye. Now I'm getting a dozen texts a day about you. I must say, I was dying to meet you."

Jack blushed. "Tess is quite a woman." He glanced

over to the kitchen. "I'm still waiting to wake up from this dream, because she's perfect."

"Oh, well I'd be happy to tell you about her many flaws. Let the nightmare begin," Omar jested.

"I heard that," Tess called, carrying four champagne flutes on a tray, three with mimosas and one sparkling water, which she placed on the coffee table.

"I'm impressed, Butterfly. If this writing thing doesn't work out, maybe we can get you a job at a saloon."

"I do love a good peasant skirt," she said, knuckling the top of his head and tussling his hair.

"Now I'm going to have bad hair all day," he complained.

"Serves you right," she said, plopping down beside Jack.

"We were just getting ready to tell Jack about your flaws," Omar said. "Where shall we begin?"

"Clay, was I this terrible when I first met you?" Tess asked.

"No, you weren't. You were the epitome of grace and kindness," Clay replied.

"I'm just teasing," Omar said, smiling at Tess. He turned his attention to Jack. "Truly, we're so happy to meet you."

"Tess said that you two have been friends since college, but she didn't mention how you met," Jack replied.

"Everyone, please take some food," Tess interjected.

They all helped themselves to the artichoke and tomato frittata and green bean salad.

"Tess and I met on our first day of college. It was orientation day, where they put you in groups and try to force you to bond. Then there was a cookout. At the end of the compulsory festivities, a bunch of kids decided to go hang out on the football field. Tess and I both ended up there. Someone was blasting music and most of the kids were smoking pot, but since that wasn't our scene, Tess and I wandered off together and lay down at the other end of the field, looking at the stars. We didn't even know each other, but we just started talking and something clicked. She told me that she was writing a novel and that I was the only person she had told. And I swear to you, she was barely eighteen years old, but I knew she was serious, that she was the real deal. I remember telling her the novel was going to be extraordinary."

Tess leaned against Jack, and he rubbed her arm.

Omar continued, "And then I revealed that I was gay and that she was the only person I had ever told. In my family and culture, it's a crime. She said that life is so unfair and it's especially hard with family because even when they disappoint us to the core, we still long for their love and approval. Then she said I was a beautiful person and deserved to live my life fully and authentically. So strange to think about it now, how much trust we had for each other in a matter of moments." Omar watched Tess and Jack with a soft smile on his face. "Sometimes it happens quickly, I suppose. We just know who the good souls are."

They continued eating and talking for over an hour. Eventually, Tess said, "I'm going to make tea and get dessert."

Clay stood up. "I'll help."

When they walked out of the room, Omar quietly said, "That woman hasn't eaten dessert in twenty years, but she always makes sure her guests have everything."

"She's hard on herself," Jack said.

Omar nodded. "If only she could extend to herself what she gives so freely to others."

Soon, Clay returned with a pot of tea and four teacups. Tess placed a platter of bite-size lemon bars, oatmeal raspberry bars, and brownies on the coffee table. "Please, help yourselves," she said.

"The hostess first. Tess, would you like something?" Jack asked.

"I never eat sweets, but all right, just a little," she replied, leaning over and selecting an oatmeal raspberry bite, which she promptly nibbled on. "Ooh, that's good. You should try one."

Omar looked at Clay in disbelief.

Jack rubbed Tess's back and said, "Omar was just about to tell me a funny story about when you two worked in your school cafeteria."

"I can't leave you two alone for a second," Tess replied.

"Oh, come on, you did look fetching in that orange smock," Omar joked.

"Not as good as you looked in your hairnet," Tess quipped.

"That was certainly a confidence killer. Bloody thing ruined my dating life," Omar groaned. "But beggars can't be choosers. With huge student loans, no family support to speak of, and not a nickel between us, we both needed that dreadful job."

"True. At least we had each other," Tess said.

"Always," Omar agreed.

"And we made the most of it," Tess continued.

"Indeed," Omar said. His voice slowed as he added, "Funny how when you find your people, life just gets easier, even when it's hard."

Tess and Omar smiled at each other as she nestled into Jack.

An hour later, Omar and Clay were leaving.

"Tess, you were so sweet to make artichokes. You know they're my favorite," Clay said.

"My pleasure," she replied, hugging him. "Thank you so much for coming over."

"Really great to meet you, Jack," Omar said. He hugged Tess and whispered, "He's wonderful, Butterfly. Be happy."

She smiled and said, "Talk to you tomorrow no doubt, and I'll see you Thursday for our usual breakfast."

"I'll be there with bells on."

After they left, Tess put her arms around Jack's neck. "They loved you, like I knew they would."

"They're terrific. I like the way Omar teases you."

"Oh please, don't encourage him."

Jack laughed. "Why does he call you Butterfly?"

"No idea. He's been doing it since we graduated from college. I never asked why."

Chapter 3

"Hello, Ms. Lee," Alfred said with a smile as Tess approached the host stand.

"Good morning, Alfred. How are you on this lovely day?"

"Very well, thank you."

"How's your wife doing since her little fall?"

"Much better. It was just a minor sprain. Thank you for asking. Your guest is waiting for you. Please follow me," he said.

As they walked through the grand hotel dining room, Tess looked around as if she had not seen it every week since moving to the area, admiring the glossy wood floors, massive windows with cobalt velvet drapes, and the usual smattering of politicians to whom she politely nodded hello. When she arrived at their regular corner table, Omar jumped up to greet her. They embraced and then plopped down in their leather captain chairs.

"This place is so DC," Tess remarked.

"Tell me about it. I always feel conspicuous sitting here without a work project or urgent phone call. Like I should be schmoozing the room, or some such thing. Honestly, I don't know how these Washington people plaster those over-the-top smiles on all day. It looks bloody exhausting."

Tess giggled, unable to stop a smile from spreading across her own face. Before Omar could comment, their waitress came over with a sterling silver coffee pot.

"Good morning, Ms. Lee. Would you like some French roast?" she asked.

"Yes, please. Thank you, Bridget," Tess replied.

"Are you both having the usual today?"

"I am. Thank you," Tess replied.

Omar nodded and Bridget scurried away.

"They do have the most divine crab Benedict. Must say, I would miss that if we changed our breakfast spot to somewhere less . . ." Omar trailed off as if searching for the right word.

"Less austere? Less see-and-be-seen? Less top-shelf-booze and back-room-deal?" she joked.

He chuckled. "Indeed. Or how's this? Less politico-with-a-prostitute-in-his-penthouse."

"Good one," Tess remarked, and they both laughed. "Well, besides your Benedict addiction, they do always make me plain poached eggs without hassling me. The beauty of hotels. They're accommodating."

"I don't want to go all head shrink and bug you, but how's your eating these days?" he asked.

"Fine. You don't need to worry. I bring a snack with me everywhere like you suggested so I don't forget to eat, and I've been a lot less rigid. I can't remember the last time I purposely skipped a meal. Now that I have someone to cook for, it's different. Everything is different," she said, breaking out into a huge smile. "So, I can't believe you haven't said anything yet. Aren't you going to tell me what you think about Jack?"

"Holy hotness, Butterfly. He's sexy as all hell. You can literally see the curves of his pecs and his biceps through his shirt."

She giggled.

"I'm telling you, my first thought was 'Holy shit, he's a real-life G.I. Joe doll.' God, did I have a fondness for those figurines. Still have these erotic military dreams from time to time. Don't tell Clay."

Her giggle morphed into laughter. "Let me guess, you're some low-level army private cleaning the latrine when a hot sergeant you're in lust with comes in to have his way with you."

"Why do you assume I'm the private and not the sergeant?"

She furrowed her brow.

"Fine, you're exactly right," he said with a dramatic eye roll, "but it's the kitchen not the latrine, and the whole lot of fellow privates are right outside the door in the mess hall. We could be caught at any moment, which is quite the aphrodisiac."

She laughed.

"Enough of that, back to your hot man. Please tell me you're having mind-blowing sex," he teased.

"We are," she said, crinkling her nose and smiling mischievously.

"I think about all the men who pursued you over the years—the rock stars, athletes, businessmen, not to mention that royal." Tess rolled her eyes and Omar continued, "Who knew, all this time you were waiting for the strong and silent type."

"Funny you put it that way. For as long as I can remember, I've clung to words like a life raft. But when Jack and I are together, it's like we don't need them at all. We feel so much. It's unspoken. Words aren't necessary." Omar smiled and she continued, "Somehow, we just connect and understand each other in a powerful way."

"I'm so happy for you I don't even have the words for it myself. When I saw you two together, it was clear you're meant for one another. I've never seen you so at ease."

"I've never felt this way before. It's the best feeling in the world." She paused and added, "You like him, right?"

"Very much. It's obvious he's one of the good ones."

She beamed. "From the moment we met, something inside of me knew I could trust him entirely. Just like when you and I met." She lowered her voice and said, "Omar, I told him about my childhood. Our first night together."

"Wow, you've never told any of your lovers anything about your past."

"It's different with Jack. I know it seems impossible after such a short time, but we're so close. We accept each other completely, scars and all. No questions. And . . ." She stopped as her eyes misted.

"What, Butterfly?" he asked gently.

"It's like I told you on the phone after our first weekend together. He sees me. Not who my family said I was. Not Tess Lee either. Me. Just me."

Omar reached his hand across the table and put it over hers. "Lean into it."

She sniffled, squeezed his hand, and then wiped her eyes. "I am."

Just then Bridget returned and served their meals.

Omar picked up his fork and knife and said, "Well, this looks scrumptious. Now I know Jack has depth, sensitivity, intelligence, blah, blah, blah. But right now, who cares about any of that. While I indulge myself, I want to hear all the juicy stuff. Tell me everything about your sexcapades with your very own American hero."

Chapter 4

The following night, Jack and Tess had plans for all their closest friends to meet each other. Jack, Joe, Bobby, and Gina arrived at Shelby's Bar first, followed by Tess. Shortly after, Omar and Clay joined them. Tess and Jack made the introductions and ordered the first round of drinks. Soon, they were all telling stories and laughing like old friends.

"Gina's family doesn't mess around. Italian food is like their religion. Basically, you eat until you drop. Her mother serves all the guys like three huge slabs of lasagna, and you eat them even if you think you might burst," Bobby said, exploding into laughter.

Gina playfully hit his arm as the others laughed.

"Come on, who's next?" Bobby asked.

"I have one," Joe said. "It was during college. I went on a few dates with this student from Sweden. Blonde hair, blue eyes, beautiful girl. I was smitten. Her parents visited, and she invited me to dinner at her apartment to meet them. They served things I had never even heard of, starting with pickled herring." Bobby groaned and Joe continued,

"I wanted to be courteous, but let's just say, if you're not accustomed to that food, it's jolting."

"Did you manage to eat it?" Jack asked.

"I did my best. Took small bites and tried to swallow them whole, like I was taking medicine. Like I always say, when a beautiful woman asks you to do something, just do it. Or try at least."

Jack smiled and draped his arm around Tess.

Tess giggled and Omar said, "Butterfly, perhaps I should tell one of our tales."

"We never had to introduce anyone to our families, or anything like that, thank goodness," she replied with a shrug.

"But there was that time in Ethiopia," he said, raising his eyebrows.

Tess made a face. "That was unfortunate."

"Indeed it was," Omar agreed.

"Do you still hold that against me?"

"Do I ever hold anything against you? But bloody hell, I do make sure everyone knows your food preferences," he replied, lightheartedly lobbing a pretzel at her.

"This sounds good. Tell us," Jack said.

"It was years ago," Omar began. "Tess was invited to the opening of a girls' school because she had funded their . . ."

"Hey, now," Tess interrupted, grabbing a pretzel from the bowl and flinging it at him. "There's no need to make a fuss about why I was there. Just tell them about the dinner."

"Bloody hell, how can anyone be so modest about their good deeds?" Tess stared him down and he conceded, "All right, my ever humble one. Just remember, it's your fault I got sick. Perhaps you could allow me the fun of making you cringe while I relay the details."

"Fair enough," she said with a shrug.

"Anyway," Omar continued, "to thank Tess for her generosity, the hosts surprised us with this extraordinary feast. In Ethiopia instead of utensils you take injera, which is this kind of fermented, sour, spongy bread, sort of like flatbread, and you use it to scoop up various dishes. Tess almost never eats bread—"

"Well, I would have in this case to be polite," she interjected.

"Yes, but sadly everything else was meat based. Many different spiced beef and lamb dishes. Tess is a vegetarian. She took one look at the long table brimming with bowls and platters overflowing with meat . . . I thought she might be sick."

"I felt terrible. These people were so incredibly kind and generous to us, and food is scarce there, and they prepared this enormous, extravagant spread in our honor. I wanted to be polite, but I could never bring myself to eat meat."

"So, what did you do?" Joe asked.

"I looked at Omar and . . ."

"And I ate enough for the both of us, and then some," Omar said. "Tess kept discretely moving food from her plate to mine."

"Was it good?" Jack asked.

"Delicious. Some of the tastiest food I had ever eaten. But either something was bad or just the sheer quantity alone was too much because I wound up sick as a dog. Literally couldn't leave the bathroom for days. We had to extend our trip. Felt off for a week."

"It really was terrible. I felt so bad for you. Luckily, I was fine," Tess said with a giggle.

"Yeah, luckily," Omar said, flinging another pretzel at her.

As the night progressed, Gina and the guys shared a few platters of chicken wings and Tess picked at a Caprese salad.

"That's a pretty necklace," Gina said to Tess.

"Thank you. I wear it every day. It was a gift from Jack," she replied, cozying up against him.

Jack noticed a Middle Eastern man pacing and staring at them from a few feet away, and when they made eye contact, the man approached the table.

He walked up to Omar and asked, "Pardon me, do you speak Arabic?"

"Yes," Omar replied.

He spoke to Omar in Arabic and kept glancing over at Tess. Omar said something in reply and then turned to Tess. "His wife would like to speak to you," he said, gesturing to a woman at a table in the corner. "She doesn't speak English, so he asked me to translate. If you don't want to, it's fine. I'll tell him. You don't have to do this."

Tess looked over at the woman, studying her. "It's okay. I'll talk to her."

Omar relayed the message, and then he and Tess stood up.

"Please excuse us," Tess said, and she and Omar walked over and joined the woman at her table.

"I wonder what that's about," Bobby said.

"It seemed to me like maybe Omar didn't want Tess to go. Am I wrong, Clay?" Joe asked.

Clay shrugged. "I'm not sure. He's very protective of her."

Jack didn't take his eyes off Tess. She spoke with the woman for ten minutes, and then they embraced. The couple left. Tess walked toward the restrooms, and Omar returned to the table.

"Where's Tess?" Jack asked.

"She needed a minute," Omar replied.

"What's going on?" Jack asked.

"I'm sure you all know about Tess's publishing deal and how she owns all the rights to her books, including translation rights. The media wrote all kinds of stories about what a fierce negotiator she is and that her goal was to create a bidding war and raise the price for licensing her work."

Joe nodded. "I read about it at the time."

"Me too," Gina said.

"Tess believes that charity is something you shouldn't shine a spotlight on, so she never corrected the media, but accumulating wealth wasn't her primary motivation. The first thing she did was to give translation rights to nearly every publisher in the Middle East for free. No licensing fees, no royalties, she just gave her work away. She made sure the rights were nonexclusive, so that any publisher who wanted to print and distribute the books would be able to do so, with profit as their motivation. She knew that would flood the market, and hopefully the books would find their way into the hands of those who needed them."

Jack inhaled. "Wow."

"That's truly remarkable," Joe said.

"That's just who Tess is," Omar replied. "But there has been a price to pay. She made some very powerful enemies, as well as scores of brutes who are just plain scary and aren't too keen on women's stories of resilience ending up in the hands and minds of girls and women in their countries."

"Yeah, I bet," Joe said.

"But she expected that type of trouble and doesn't pay any attention to it, even when she should. What she didn't anticipate was what those books would mean to the women who found them. I traveled with her through the Middle East, and you just can't imagine some of the stories that women would tell her about their lives, how they read her books in secret, and what her words mean to them. Even at Heathrow Airport or JFK, women have approached her in public restrooms to share their distressing personal stories. The woman she just spoke with is from Afghanistan. She told Tess about the daughter of a friend . . . she was raped by five men. I won't go into all the details, but it was difficult to hear. Before she left, she thanked Tess for her books, told her how much strength and encouragement they provide, and asked her to please keep writing."

"Is Tess okay?" Jack asked.

"She used to hear these kinds of stories many times a day. She had ways of dealing with it, things she would do to prepare herself to hear the horrors of the world. Of course, each person thinks only of their desire to share their own story, and not the cumulative burden placed on Tess to take in so many people's trauma. I always felt it was terribly unfair of people, but of course Tess is too generous to see things that way. To her, it's like a duty, an ethical obligation or something. About a year ago, she informed everyone she worked with that she wasn't going to do any more public appearances. No explanation. I don't think anything changed; she just decided she was done. But since then, she has a very difficult time when readers approach her, maybe because she hasn't done the mental or spiritual work to prepare for it. I don't know. I just know it hurts her. But still, she won't turn anyone away unless she has a bad feeling about them, and then she won't even shake their hand. It's like she sees something in people's eyes and doesn't know how to look away. She just can't look away. It's some kind of deep-seated call to humanize everyone. It's hard to explain until you see it for yourself." Omar noticed Tess was on her way back to the table. "Please don't say anything. She doesn't like to talk about it."

Everyone nodded.

Tess sat down in the booth next to Jack. He put his hand on her thigh and whispered, "You okay?"

"Yeah." She turned her attention to the table. "So Bobby, you were going to teach me how to play darts."

✦ ✦ ✦

"You're getting better," Bobby said a half hour later.

Tess laughed. "I'm terrible, but it's fun."

"I'm not very good either," Gina said, picking up another dart and shooting it at the edge of the board.

"No, you're not," Bobby agreed with a laugh.

Tess glanced over and saw Jack watching them.

Gina noticed and said, "He's so crazy about you."

"The feeling is mutual," Tess replied.

"We're all so happy for him. He's the greatest, most patriotic guy. He was alone for so long, and then after Gracie, we thought we'd never see him smile again," Gina said.

A look of confusion washed across Tess's face.

"Gina," Bobby mumbled.

"Oh my God, I'm so sorry. I just assumed he told you," Gina stammered.

Bobby looked at Tess. "Gracie was Jack's daughter. She died about eight months ago. I'm sure he was planning to tell you, but it's really hard for him. Here's a guy who devoted his entire life to protecting strangers, but he couldn't save his own daughter. It tortures him."

Tess was stunned but managed to say, "That's okay. Please don't say anything to him." They played darts for a little longer until Tess heard the DJ put on Lady Gaga and Bradley Cooper's "Shallow."

"Excuse me," she said, and she walked over to Jack. She took his hand. "It's a slow one. Dance with me?"

He got up and followed her to the dance floor. They pressed their bodies together, melting into each other. When the song was over, Tess whispered, "Let's stay at your place tonight."

✦ ✦ ✦

When they got to Jack's apartment, he went to grab a couple glasses of water. Tess sat down on the couch and noticed a pile of her books on the coffee table.

Jack sat down next to her. "I ordered your books."

"Yeah, I can see that."

"I've been reading them on my lunch break. I'm on the second one. Tess, you're so talented. They're incredible. Powerful. Brave. Honest. Hopeful. I'm in awe."

She smiled.

"It's beautiful how you always use the same dedication, 'To everyone, everywhere.'"

"Every time I start a book, I'm writing it for myself, but somewhere along the way I realize I'm writing it for everyone else too. Anyone who needs it at least."

"That's sweet, and so you," he said. "I was surprised you wanted to stay here tonight. We've been at your place all week."

"I thought you might be more comfortable," she explained, putting her hand on his thigh. "I need to talk to you about something."

He took her hands in his. "What is it?"

"Gina told me about Gracie. She didn't mean to. She didn't realize I didn't know."

Jack looked down and took a deep breath. "I'm sorry," he said. "I . . . I wasn't trying to keep it from you. It's just that it's so hard to talk about."

"You don't have to be sorry. Do you want to tell me now?"

He took a moment to gather himself, and then he began. "Until I took a desk job about a year ago, I didn't think I could be in a relationship. My job was too intense, too dangerous, too unpredictable. But sometimes I'd meet someone in a bar for a night. That's how I met her mother. It was just one night, five years ago. She never told me she was pregnant. I didn't know I was a father until about eight months ago when she contacted me. She told me about Gracie and that she was sick." He stopped as his eyes flooded with tears. Tess rubbed his back. He wiped the tears away and continued. "She had leukemia and needed a bone marrow transplant. Her mother wanted me to get tested." He paused and took a breath. "But she was too sick. It was too late. There was nothing they could do. I spent eleven days in the hospital with her, and then she died. I only knew her for eleven days, and she didn't even know who I was." He began sobbing.

"You said you once took two weeks off from work. That was why," Tess said.

"Yes," he mumbled through his tears. "I slept at the hospital for eleven days, by her side."

"I'm so sorry, Jack. What was Gracie like?"

"She was an angel. She loved the color purple, and she had the sweetest laugh."

"Do you have a picture of her?"

He got up and went into his bedroom. He returned with two photographs.

"She's beautiful," Tess said.

"She didn't look like this when I knew her. She was so frail and had lost her hair, but she was still beautiful. Her mother gave me these so I could see what she had been like."

"Do you keep in touch with her mother?"

He shook his head. "At first, I was furious with her. Overwhelmed by anger. But then I realized, I realized . . ."

She rubbed his back. "What?"

"It was my fault, it was all my fault," he said, doubling over and bursting into tears.

"It wasn't your fault, Jack. Why do you think that?"

"She never told me about Gracie because she didn't want me in their lives. I never led anyone on or treated anyone badly, but I must have done something wrong because she never even told me she was pregnant. Maybe it was because of my stupid job; I told her how dangerous it was and that's why I couldn't have relationships. But it was my fault, my fault she didn't want me to know about her or be in her life. It was my fault she didn't tell me in time so that I could save her," he said, his body rocking back and forth as he sobbed.

"Oh, baby, it wasn't your fault. It wasn't your fault. You didn't do anything wrong." He couldn't stop crying. Tess threw her arms around him. "I've got you. It's okay. I've got you."

A few minutes later, Jack was finally able to take a deep breath and stop crying. He wiped his eyes and looked up at Tess. "I never thought I could have this kind of happiness until I met you, especially after Gracie. I love you with all my heart, and I don't ever want to lose you. I'll do anything for you."

"Jack, I never truly felt safe or at peace until I met you. You're everything to me. I'm right here, and I'm not going anywhere."

Chapter 5

After spending every night together, Jack and Tess met their friends at Shelby's Bar the next Friday night, taking what had already become their usual table by the dance floor. They spent the evening talking and laughing like they had all known each other for years.

Tess noticed that Omar kept checking his phone and seemed disconnected from the group. She picked up a pretzel, tossed it at him, and said, "All work and no play makes Omar a big bore."

"He's worse than I am when I'm on call," Clay said.

Omar shot them each a look.

"I was promised a night of fun and dancing. I don't care about anything else," Tess said, picking up another pretzel and flinging it at him.

Omar intercepted it midair. "If you do that again, you're going to wear that basket," he teased.

"See, isn't this more fun than staring at your phone?" Tess asked, smiling playfully.

"Butterfly, I'm doing this for you. The final offer is going to come in any minute, and I promised I'd get a response from you right away," Omar said. "Ah, and here it is!" He put his phone down and looked at Tess. "They're up to $5.5 million, plus a cut of merchandising, and they're still offering a producer credit, although I know you're not interested. It's an A-level deal. This is as good as it gets. I spoke with Larry directly. He wants this to happen; he's already clearing space on his mantel for the awards."

"Is he?" Tess asked.

"Everyone is hoping you'll give the green light before the weekend."

"It's already the weekend," Tess protested.

"They're on LA time."

Tess picked up a pretzel and started picking off the grains of salt, one by one.

"Butterfly, you know I wouldn't press you, but this has dragged on for ages and we can finally close it. No one will be comfortable until you give the word. They know how you are."

She shot him a look.

"What is it?" Omar asked.

"I don't like this bleeding into my time with Jack and our friends."

"Then why didn't you accept the offer they made two days ago, or the one this morning? We both know this will end with a phone call between you and Larry anyway. You could have called him earlier."

"That offer wasn't a good starting point for the conversation. Besides, maybe I don't want to do it at all."

Omar sighed. "If that's really the case, I'll tell them to fuck off."

"You would not," Tess said gleefully.

"If that's what you want, yes I would. Just say the word."

Tess picked up another pretzel, rolling it around in her fingers.

"Please call Larry. He's at the office with his legal team on standby. You do know he's the head of a major studio, right, Butterfly? He doesn't wait around for most people."

Tess nuzzled closer to Jack.

Omar raised his eyebrows, silently prodding her.

"You're impossible. Okay, I'll call him." She looked up at Jack. "I'm sorry, baby. I'll be right back."

He kissed her, and she excused herself from the table.

Omar turned to Clay. "She's not going to accept the deal. I could see it in her eyes when I said the number. It's a world-class offer." He looked at Jack. "I'm sorry. It's my fault. She never conducts business when she's with friends. Bloody hell, we can't even get her to answer her cell phone, which is maddening. I'm sure she'll give me grief later."

"It's fine," Jack said. "Tess can do whatever she needs to do. What's it all about, anyway?"

"It's for the film rights to one of her books. We've worked with this studio before. We have a good relationship with them, and it will be worth the licensing price many times over once you consider the ripple effect."

"That's so exciting," Gina gushed. "I've seen all the movies they've adapted from her books. *Blue Moon* is my favorite movie of all time. Does Tess have a favorite?"

Omar laughed. "She's never seen any of them."

"Are you serious?" Joe asked.

"Yeah. If you ask her, she'll tell you that she doesn't have to see the film because she's read the book."

Jack laughed.

"Tess has a very personal relationship with her books. She rarely discusses the characters and what they mean to her. I think she prefers to let them live in her imagination as she created them," Omar said.

"Tell me . . . Tess is so sweet. Do people try to take advantage of her?" Jack asked.

"I pity anyone who does," Omar replied with a chuckle and a shake of his head. "Her debut novel became an international bestseller when she was barely twenty-two. Within a year, she was signing her landmark publishing deal, for which she was the sole architect. Afterward, she put together a small team of advisers and asked me to be there for support. She asked a trademark lawyer to explain some specifics to her, but instead of explaining, he tried to tell her what to do. She said, 'I'm not asking for your advice; I'm asking for an education.' He countered that he didn't want to waste time. She told him, 'I have time and I'm paying for your time. What's the issue? Do you think you're not capable of teaching me, or that I'm not capable of learning?' Before he could respond, she calmly said, 'Thank you, but your services are no longer needed.' He was floored. She set the tone then and there. And I'll tell you, now that woman knows more about intellectual property law than most attorneys."

Jack laughed.

Omar continued, "Many people tried to convince her to focus on her art and leave the business to others, but she was having none of it. She didn't want to be at the mercy of the men who run this industry. Anyone who ever suggested that she couldn't be both a great artist and a fierce businesswoman was sorely mistaken. If you ever want to see something truly impressive, watch her run a meeting. She never loses her kindness, but she's in complete control. Just the other day, we were having our weekly video conference with her team. Someone made a suggestion that she didn't agree with. After hearing them out, she calmly but firmly said no. A few minutes later, he attempted to repackage his advice. She stopped him and said, 'I already said no. No is a complete sentence.' When the meeting was over, she dissolved any lingering tension by asking about his wife, who recently got a promotion. No one takes advantage of Tess, nor does she ever lose herself."

Jack smiled.

Omar took a swig of his drink and continued, "I'll bet you that right now, she's either breaking Larry's heart by turning down the deal or she's getting the price up. Either way, I guarantee that she asks about his kids. Of course, she only cares about the price because she's planning to give it all away, otherwise it wouldn't matter to her. Tess's only blind spot is self-care. When she first started touring, she had a laundry list of requirements. There had to be access for people with disabilities anywhere she spoke, she insisted on being interviewed by people of color, and on and on. But she wouldn't put simple things like water in her rider. One convention manager actually had to ask, 'Does Ms. Lee want something to drink in the greenroom?' I asked Tess and she was like, 'Oh yeah, water would be fine.' I asked her what kind, and she said it didn't matter. That's when I decided to travel with her whenever possible, so I could look out for her."

"Have you ever regretted changing your life that way?" Jack asked.

"Not for a second. Tess leads an extraordinary life, and I've been lucky to be a part of it. My only regret is that I've enjoyed it more than she has."

The conversation moved on, and fifteen minutes later, Tess returned to the table. She slid back into the booth beside Jack, who draped his arm around her. "I missed you," she whispered.

"I missed you too," he replied.

Everyone stared at her expectantly. Omar's eyes were like saucers. "Well?" he asked.

"Seven point two, plus a cut of merchandising," she said matter-of-factly.

Omar grinned from ear to ear. He raised his glass. Tess picked up her glass and they clinked. "Holy hell, you are brilliant, Butterfly. How did you possibly manage that?"

Tess's expression turned serious. "Perhaps I told him he was buying a piece of my soul, and I asked him what he might consider a fair price for a piece of his soul."

Omar furrowed his brow, picked up a pretzel, and lobbed it at her. "How did you really do it?"

Tess smirked. "At my suggestion, they're going to donate twenty percent of it to a mutually agreed upon charity, which is a great tax break for them and good PR. We'll match the donation."

Omar laughed. "Well done."

"Oh, and he said hi to you," Tess added. "His older daughter decided to major in psychology. I told him you'd be a resource."

Omar glanced at Jack, and they both smiled.

"Am I off the clock now? Have I sufficiently earned my keep?" Tess asked.

"Does this mean it's a bad time to ask if you've reconsidered the invitation to judge that beauty pageant?" Omar joked.

Tess got ready to throw the whole basket of pretzels.

He laughed. "Yes, Butterfly. You're free."

"Good, because I was promised a night of dancing, and so far, there has been no dancing."

Everyone congratulated Tess on the deal, and the conversation moved on. Jack leaned over and whispered, "Come with me." He took Tess's hand and led her to the hallway near the restrooms, the quietest spot in the bar.

"What you said to Omar was true; I could hear it in your voice. That's how you feel when you sell your work, like you're selling a piece of your soul."

Her eyes became watery. "Yes," she said softly.

He pulled her close, holding her in a comforting embrace.

"Jack?"

"Yeah, baby?"

She gazed into his eyes and asked, "Do you think it's possible for two people to know each other completely?"

"Yes, I do," he replied, brushing the side of her face.

✦ ✦ ✦

When the DJ showed up, Tess, Gina, and Clay got up to dance. The others watched as the trio let loose to a string of pub favorites. Eventually, they tired and rejoined the group. Tess cozied up to Jack.

"Jack, you're as bad as Bobby. He won't dance with me either. Thank God for Clay," Gina said.

"I stick to the slow songs," Jack replied.

When the unmistakable opening piano notes of "All of Me" came on, Tess looked up at Jack. "It's our song, baby."

"That's my cue," he said to the group.

He led her onto the dance floor. She put one hand on his shoulder, and he slipped one around her waist to the small of her back. They started to sway, staring at each other as if they were the only people in the world. As the song progressed, she moved her hand down his arm to pull him closer, and he ran his fingers through her hair. They were pressed tightly together, in slow movement. Everyone at their table watched, smiles across their faces.

"Whoa," Bobby mumbled.

"They are really in love. I've never seen anything like it," Joe said.

Clay put his arm around Omar and said, "Look at them."

"If I didn't see it with my own eyes, I'd never believe it. My sweet Butterfly is truly happy."

When the song was over, Jack whispered, "Let's go to your place."

✦ ✦ ✦

At the end of the evening, they all bundled up and stumbled out of the bar.

A homeless man standing on the sidewalk asked, "Can you please spare anything?"

The group stood around awkwardly, but Tess walked right up to him. "Hi. I'm Tess, this is Jack, and these are our friends."

Jack stepped directly behind Tess in a protective stance.

"What's your name?" Tess gently asked the man.

"Henry," he replied.

She smiled, pulled a twenty-dollar bill out of her pocket, and handed it to him. When he took the money, she held his hand. Surprised, he looked at her and said, "You're very kind. Thank you."

"Getting kind of cold out," she remarked, still holding his hand.

"Sure is."

She took off her cashmere scarf and held it out. "Here, please take this and try to stay warm."

"Wow," Joe muttered.

"Oh, I couldn't," Henry said.

"Please, I insist."

"Thank you," he said, taking the scarf. "Someone must have taught you to do unto others."

"No, someone taught me there are no others. Good night, Henry."

She turned to her friends, their mouths agape.

Henry looked at Jack, who hadn't moved, and quietly asked, "Is she some kind of angel?"

"Yeah, something like that," he muttered.

Tess walked over to Omar and hugged him. "Our usual breakfast on Thursday?"

"Yes, Butterfly."

"Good night, guys," she said to her friends.

They all said goodbye. Jack took Tess's hand and walked her to his car. He opened her door and she got in. When he closed the door, he looked back at Henry, who was wrapping the scarf around his neck and smiling.

✦ ✦ ✦

Tess removed her coat and shoes as Jack locked the door. He kicked off his shoes and threw his jacket on the countertop. He came up behind Tess and slipped his hands around her waist, and she turned to face him. Without a word, they started to kiss passionately. He picked her up, carried her to the bedroom, and put her down on the edge of the bed. They both pulled their shirts off. Jack grabbed a pillow and placed it behind Tess. He laid her down, pulled off the rest of her clothes, and took off his own. Starting at her feet, he gently kissed her, working his way up her body. Soon, they were making love, screaming in bliss. Afterward, they lay beside each other, kissing. Jack pulled a blanket over them.

"I'm sorry," he said, stroking her cheek. "I couldn't wait another minute."

"I'm so happy. I've never felt anything like this before."

"Me either."

"I have this big house, but I've never in my life felt like I've had a home. Being with you feels like home."

"To me too," he said.

"Why don't you move in with me? I want to wake up each morning with you and fall asleep in your arms each night."

"Marry me, Tess."

"Are you serious?"

"I've never been more serious in my life. I love you with my whole heart, forever. Marry me."

"Yes," she whispered. "I'll marry you."

Chapter 6

Jack pulled into a parking space outside the restaurant. "Ready? The gang is probably here."

"Do you think Omar will be happy for us?" Tess asked, fidgeting. She was obviously nervous.

"I hope so."

"But what if he isn't?" she asked, her delicate face marred with distress.

"How he feels about it means a lot to you."

"Yes. I would be heartbroken if . . ."

He squeezed her hand. "I promise I'll do everything I can to show him how much I love you."

She took a deep breath. "Okay, let's go."

The waitress served their drinks and asked, "Are you ready to order?"

"I think we need a few more minutes," Jack replied.

Omar held up his mimosa. "Brunch is my favorite meal."

"That's because it's just breakfast with cocktails," Tess said from across the table.

"Exactly," he agreed.

"Brunch is my favorite too. This place is really cute. We've never been here before," Gina said, touching Bobby's hand.

"I've been coming here for years and suggested it when Jack texted. Glad you like it," Joe said.

"Clay sends his regrets. Life of a surgeon, you know. So Tess, to what do we owe? Twice in one weekend. When you invited us to brunch, you said you had news. Something we can toast to?" Omar asked.

"As a matter of fact, yes," she replied. She turned to Jack. "Go ahead."

He slung his arm around her. "We're getting married."

"Oh my God, that's so exciting!" Gina exclaimed.

"Wow, congratulations," Joe said.

"Yeah, wow. Congratulations, you two," Bobby said, raising his glass. "That's awesome."

"Omar?" Tess asked, her eyebrows raised.

"Oh, Butterfly, I'm so happy for you," he gushed, jumping up and rushing over to hug her. "You're perfect for each other," he whispered. When he finally let go of Tess, Jack stood up and shook his hand.

"Congratulations. You're a lucky man," Omar said.

"Thank you. I know it."

When they all sat down, Omar raised his glass. "Well, this is certainly worthy of a toast. To Tess and Jack! I wish you every happiness."

"Cheers!"

"So? When's the big day?" Joe asked.

"Saturday," Tess replied.

Omar choked on his drink. "Saturday, as in six days from now?"

"Yes, so I'll need your help," Tess replied.

"Butterfly, I know you're a writer, but must everything always be so dramatic? Why so fast?" Omar asked.

She rolled her eyes. "Because we've already waited a lifetime. It's going to be small, at our place, a private ceremony at five o'clock followed by a cocktail party at eight. We're only having about forty or fifty people. I already called the long-distance guests yesterday . . . Crystal is booking flights and hotels and making arrangements for those flying private. But I could really use your help. Since Clay is at the hospital today, we were hoping you could come over after brunch. Pretty please?"

Omar smiled. "Of course. Whatever you need."

"Oh, and don't flip out, but I'm legally changing my name," Tess said.

"Your publisher will love that," Omar joked.

Tess crinkled her nose. "Relax, I'll still use Tess Lee for work. But Omar, I'll finally have a real name."

He smiled.

"What do you mean?" Bobby asked.

"She was born Esther Leopold. Her family called her Essie," Omar explained.

Tess shuddered. "I hated it. When I left home, I changed it to Tess Lee. But now I'll be Tess Miller, except on my books."

"You better lead with that when you tell your publisher," Omar said.

Tess giggled.

After the waitress took their orders, a tall, thin woman with straggly brown hair approached their table. "Excuse me, are you Tess Lee?" she asked.

Everyone turned to look.

Jack put his arm across the back of Tess's chair.

"Yes," Tess replied.

"I don't want to bother you, but . . ." she said nervously.

"You're not bothering me," Tess assured her.

The woman's eyes became teary. "I've read all your novels. The last one, *Shadows*," she said, pausing before continuing, "that scene with the cereal." Her voice became quieter and more sincere. "There was a time I felt that way. Things are better now, but it's still hard sometimes. I keep that book on my nightstand. Some mornings, I reread that scene and the last line of the book. It helps me. I just wanted to say thank you."

Tess looked at her sympathetically and took the woman's hand. "You're very kind. I'm glad it helps."

When the woman walked away, Jack whispered in Tess's ear, "Are you okay?"

She just nodded.

"I haven't had a chance to read your last book yet. What scene was she talking about?" Joe asked.

"I used to hear people talk about 'good' or 'bad' times to receive news, and I always thought that was strange. Is there really a *good* time for someone to tell you that they're ill, they've cheated on you, they're an addict, someone is hurting them, or they want to die? Why is one time better than another? And so many people don't really hear the difficult things their loved ones tell them. I've always included scenes in my novels where the character is having an interior monologue about something they want to confess but never do, or scenes where someone musters the courage to share their darkest secret, but the other person doesn't truly hear them. Sometimes I set these scenes in absurd places, like a woman buying cotton candy at a carnival and revealing that her boyfriend beats her. Other times I set the scenes amid the everyday minutiae of life. As a writer, I love the small everyday stuff."

"Is that why you're so insane about refusing to get your groceries delivered or hiring a personal chef or any of the other things I've suggested to free up your time for more important matters?" Omar asked, taking a swill of his cocktail.

"How can I write about normal, daily life if I don't experience it?" Tess replied.

"Bloody hell, you've been to the grocery store before. How much do you think it's changed?" he asked with a laugh.

She shot him a look.

"Sorry, Butterfly. Please go on."

"The woman who came over was talking about a passage where the protagonist reveals something very dark, but her boyfriend is too preoccupied with his breakfast. When he finally does listen, he fails to hear the gravity of her words. I know it by heart, if you want to hear it. I remember it in detail because the moment I wrote it, I decided not to do book signings anymore."

"Please, we'd love to hear it," Joe said. Everyone else echoed their agreement.

"I'll give you a little background. The protagonist is terribly lonely. She's dating this guy, but he's kind of a loser. Their whole relationship is sad. Their apartment is sad, the sex they have is sad, even their hair is a bit dirty. There's just a veneer of sadness over everything, like a layer of grime you can't wash away. He doesn't understand who she is. She's desperate to make it work, just to have a human connection, so she summons all her courage to tell him something important. He's sitting at the Formica kitchen table, eating a bowl of Fruit Loops, and she comes in and sits across from him. The scene goes like this:

"Can you stop eating for a minute? I need to talk to you," she said.

"It'll get soggy," he responded, not even looking up from his bowl.

"I'll wait," she said. She watched him slurp each bite, listened to every munching sound, which reverberated like a jackhammer. Those minutes felt longer than all the minutes that had come before.

He finished eating, plunked his spoon down into the remnant pink milk, and looked at her. "Well? What is it?"

"Every morning when I wake up, the first thing I think to myself is: *Today I can die.* Without that thought, without knowing I can end it, I couldn't bear to get up. I lie in bed and think of all the ways I can die. First, I think that I want to crawl into a hole. No thought brings me more comfort than picturing myself buried in the ground, but I can't figure out how to do it by myself. I would fail. I can't fail again. So then, I wish my body was like a lobster's. I imagine someone splitting me down the middle, cracking my back, pulling off my limbs, and scooping out my insides. The thought brings relief, but it's unrealistic, so I start to think about things that are possible. I could get a gun, slit my wrists, or hang myself from that flickering light in the closet. But I'm a coward, this I know. Maybe I should jump off a bridge, that bridge just outside of town, the rusty one. I think it's high enough, but I'm not sure. I wonder if I'll feel my body crashing against the water. Will my bones break? And then I wonder, when I leap, should I close my eyes or keep them open? I can't decide. Until I know that, I'm stuck, so I move on with the day. Every morning, I wage this war before you even get out of bed. It always begins the same way. I think to myself, *Today I can die.*" She inhaled, her eyes wide, waiting for a response.

He sat for a moment, looking at her, and eventually said, "It would be easier to just think, *Today I can live.*"

He got up and brought his bowl to the sink. She sat dumbfounded. *Today I can live.* That thought had never occurred to her.

Jack leaned over and kissed Tess on the cheek.

"It's a wonderful novel," Gina said. "I've read it twice. They break up shortly after that scene, but the last line of the book is everything."

"What's the last line?" Joe asked.

Tess gestured at Gina that she should go ahead. "On this morning, she rose to the smell of coffee, the taste of possibility, and a singular thought: *Today I can live.*"

"Wow," Bobby muttered.

"Butterfly, I never pushed because I knew how exhausted you were at the time, your schedule was maddening, and you never listened to me when I suggested slowing down. But I've always wanted to know: Why did you stop making public appearances?" Omar asked.

"You know better than anyone what my life was like: all planes, drivers, and hotels. For so long, I avoided being still, planting roots."

"It seemed like you were on a mission," Omar said.

Tess nodded. "That's how it went in my mind too. I wanted to give everything I could."

"What happened?" Omar asked.

"The writing itself takes a toll. I feel what each character feels. Even when I move on from the book, a residue remains." Jack put his hand on her thigh, she glanced at him, and they exchanged a knowing look. She returned her attention to Omar. "Then add everything else on top of that. By the end, I thought I might shatter into a million pieces if I heard one more of their stories. You know what it was like. Hundreds of readers a day, for months on end, year after year. When I wrote the cereal scene, I knew I would hear things like what that woman said. Without you all here, it would have been more intense. I just couldn't do it anymore, even with all the tricks I had learned to cope."

"You were always far too generous with your fans," Omar said.

"Nonsense. They were generous with me. They've given me so much in this life, I wanted to give back. No one took anything from me. I willingly sacrificed pieces of myself. At least for a time." She stopped and shook her head. "Besides, so much of it never felt real to me. Being trotted out like a prize horse didn't suit me."

"What do you mean?" Joe asked.

"You should have heard the way they would introduce me at all the events, all hyperbole and nonsense. I wasn't comfortable with it. The more so-called success I attained, the worse it became."

"I know, Butterfly, but there were good things too. Some of the places we saw and the people we met. We had fun," Omar said.

"It was different when you were there," Tess replied.

Omar smiled and looked around the table. "You guys should have seen the places she held talks. The crowds stood in line for hours, waiting to see her." He turned his gaze toward Tess. "The cathedral in Barcelona was amazing, ooh, and that garden in Budapest! Or when they put you in that packed arena in Singapore, with those drones flying overhead. You must admit, there were some spectacular experiences. What was your favorite? There must have been something that felt real."

Tess laughed. "I have a favorite. You weren't there and it wasn't glamorous. It was about eight years ago. I was doing a US book tour, and we stopped in Kansas for two days. I was scheduled to do a book signing at a local independent store the first night and a public talk at the university the next day. The whole trip was a nightmare. I decided not to take my jet because I didn't want the solitude, but flying commercial turned out to be a huge mistake. There was a weather event, and the plane ride was awful. People were violently sick. I'm a highly experienced traveler, and even I wasn't doing well by the time we arrived. Then my driver informed me that almost everything was shut down because of the weather. People were advised to stay at home, but the bookstore owner decided to remain open. She had ordered crateloads of books, expecting a line out the door. I felt bad for her, so I agreed to brave the weather and do the signing. Only seven people showed up."

"Seriously?" Bobby asked.

"Yeah, literally seven people. The owner was mortified. I never cared about how many people came to anything, so it didn't bother me. I thought it was kind of great. Since there were so few people, I had plenty of time to talk with each one. There was a man named Brad, about thirty years old, and he had a copy of *Candy Floss* with him that he asked me to sign. Men don't usually approach me about that book, so I was curious, but I just signed it. He told me that he was a single father of a little girl, Ava. Her mother wasn't in the picture. Ava was obviously everything to him. He glowed when he spoke about her. He told me that she thought she was ugly and she would cry about it, which broke his heart. He didn't know what to do. At the suggestion of a friend, he read my book, and for the first time, he understood how

Ava felt and why she felt that way. He thanked me profusely and said the book made him a better father."

"That's so sweet," Jack said.

Tess nodded. "Before my talk at the university the next day, I was up at the podium making sure everything was all set. Brad walked into the auditorium holding a little girl, who was maybe four or five. I walked toward them. Ava was curled up against him, the most beautiful, most perfect child I'd ever seen. She has Down syndrome."

Everyone at the table let out an audible sigh.

"Brad said that my book helped them so much and he wanted me to meet her. He said she was shy, but when he put her down, I knelt on the floor and she leapt into my arms and hugged me tightly. *That* felt real." She paused with a wistful look in her eyes before adding, "We still keep in touch. I send them signed books. Ava's doing great."

Jack took Tess's hand under the table, massaging her fingers.

"Don't you ever miss it? The travel or meeting readers?" Bobby asked.

"I did it for them, not for me. And it was too much."

"But Butterfly, it doesn't have to be that way. Instead of spending months traveling, you could do a few signings a year if you wanted. You could choose. Heaven knows your publisher would be thrilled if you'd just do a couple of events."

"Why do you care anyway?" she asked.

"Because I don't want you to be less than you are."

Tess looked down.

Omar pressed on. "You could go to New York, your favorite city. You used to spend so much time there, you must miss it."

She shrugged. "Honestly, I don't want to sacrifice any time with Jack. Not even for a day. I hope we never spend a night apart. That's what means the most to me. Please respect that."

"I could go with you," Jack offered. "If there was something you wanted to do, I can take time off."

"This guy needs a vacation," Bobby said. "He's been a workaholic for too long."

"He's right," Joe concurred.

Tess smiled faintly.

"Promise me you'll think about it, Butterfly. It could be on your terms," Omar said.

Just then, brunch was served and everyone focused on their food. Tess picked up her fork, and Jack leaned over and whispered, "I meant what I said. It's fine if you're done with public events, but if you change your mind, I'll be there."

She smiled. "I know, and I love you."

Tess brought a pot of tea into the living room where Jack and Omar were sitting.

"Thank you so much for coming over to help," Tess said to Omar. "You're the only one who knows all the guests from my side, and you can imagine the madness with this eclectic crew. I'm going to run up to the office to print out the guest list and details."

Tess flew out of the room. As soon as she was gone, Omar said, "I'm glad we have a moment alone. I was hoping to talk to you privately."

"Okay," Jack said.

"You haven't known Tess very long, and now you're getting married, and—"

Jack interrupted him. "She was so nervous about telling you."

"Tess doesn't get nervous," Omar said.

"She did about this. Your approval means the world to her. I love her. I love her with my whole heart, and I promise I always will."

Omar shook his head. "You misunderstand. I'm truly happy for you both. I knew from the first moment I saw you two that you belong together. Anyone can see how much you love each other. I understand that it can happen quickly; I knew right away with Clay. It took me a while to convince him, but I knew."

Jack laughed.

"All I have ever wanted was for Tess to find the love that she deserves so she can finally enjoy this incredible life she has created for herself. But there's something you need to know about her."

"I'm listening."

"I don't want this to come out wrong. Tess is the strongest, most brilliant person I have ever known. But there is something fragile in her."

"I know," Jack said softly. "I see it in her eyes."

"She's hugely kind to others—but not to herself."

"Her generosity of spirit bowls me over."

Omar smiled. "They say, 'Hurt people hurt people,' but sometimes that isn't true. Sometimes people in pain are able to love others in extraordinary ways, but they aren't able to extend that same love to themselves."

"I wish I could take her pain away. Please, if there's something I can do for her, tell me."

"Tess needs someone to take care of her and look out for her so that she can soar as she's meant to. She needs to feel love, every day. I'm asking you to please do that for her."

"I promise I will."

Tess returned, a stack of papers in hand. She plopped down on the couch next to Jack and asked, "So, what have I missed?"

"We were just talking about how much we love you," Jack replied.

"Ah, well I hope you still feel that way when you see your list of tasks."

Chapter 7

Tess was in the kitchen dusting off platters when Jack came home, Joe in tow. "I missed you," she said.

"Missed you too," Jack said, giving her a delicate kiss. "Sorry we're late. I stopped to pick this up for tomorrow," he said, handing her a box with a bridal bouquet of white hydrangeas.

She beamed. "It's so beautiful. Thank you."

He took the box back and put it in the refrigerator.

"I got you a wedding present too," she said.

"You didn't have to do that," he replied, turning to face her.

"I wanted to." She took his hands, looked deeply into his eyes, and gently said, "I made a small donation to pediatric cancer research in Gracie's name. It's symbolic, really."

Jack choked back his tears and took a breath. "That's the nicest thing you could have ever given me. Thank you. I love you so much." He wiped his eyes and kissed the top of her head.

"Well, we should get some plates out. Dinner will be here soon," she said, brushing his forehead with her hand.

He sniffled and turned to Joe. "Can I get you a beer?"

"Sure," Joe replied. "Tess, are you sure you guys wouldn't rather be alone tonight?"

"Absolutely. We're just getting pizza and salad delivered. Omar will be here any minute. Please stay."

"All right," Joe said. "Thank you."

The doorbell rang. Tess hit the buzzer and opened the door for Omar, who was holding a large cake box.

"Hello, hello! The wedding cake is here," he said, kissing Tess on the cheek and whizzing past her to the refrigerator.

"You know I don't eat cake, but if any cake has ever tempted me, it's this one . . . it's beautiful," Tess said as she peered through the window at the top.

"Your guests want scrumptious cake, Butterfly, and this one delivers," Omar responded, opening the refrigerator. "Oh dear, you haven't even made room," he said, placing the box on the counter while he shuffled food around.

"Sorry, I was busy today," she replied.

"Oh yes, I heard all about your treachery. First, you threaten to fire the lawyers, and now you're giving poor Barry an ulcer. I'm telling you, that man is drinking Mylanta by the bottle."

Tess tried to make a noise and shake her head to get him to stop talking, but with his back turned, he didn't notice and continued, "Did you really have to threaten to fire him again? I mean, he is an accountant, Butterfly. Even with your usual over-the-top generosity, don't you think an anonymous eleven-million-dollar donation warranted him oh, I don't know, pausing to make sure you hadn't gone completely mad?"

"Oh, Omar," she whispered.

"Wow," Joe mumbled.

"What? Eleven million dollars?" Jack murmured. "A *small* donation?"

Tess turned to face him. His eyes flooded. In a hushed tone, she said, "It's small in comparison to what you lost. Each day you had together is worth far more than a million dollars. Maybe it will help other parents and children have more days together. Are you upset?"

"Upset?" he asked softly. He wrapped his arms around her and touched his forehead to hers. "No, sweetheart. I'm . . . I'm at a loss for words."

"My whole life is words. I'm grateful we don't need them," she replied.

He smiled through his tears and gently kissed her. Then she rested her head on his chest and cuddled into him. No sounds, no words.

"Well, this bride-to-be needs her beauty sleep," Tess said. "I'm going to bed. Thank you both for coming over. You're all set on where everything goes tomorrow?"

"Yes," Omar replied. "We'll be on top of everything. Joe and I will be here at five to be your witnesses, and then you two can spend some time together while we deal with the caterers and bartender. Oh, and I'll make sure the security guard has the guest list at the door. Don't worry, Butterfly, it's all set. Your every wish is my command. By the time you and Jack emerge at eight o'clock, everything will be perfect and you can enjoy your guests."

"Thank you. I love you," she said, hugging him. She pecked Joe on the cheek and headed to her bedroom.

"I'll be there in a few minutes, sweetheart," Jack told her.

"Good night, guys. See you tomorrow," Joe said as he left.

"Omar, can I please talk to you for a minute?" Jack asked.

"Of course. What is it?"

"Earlier, you said that Tess threatened to fire her lawyers. Why?"

Omar fidgeted and looked away.

"Please, tell me," Jack said.

"They drew up a prenuptial agreement they wanted you to sign. She went nuts. She didn't want you to know about it."

"Do you have it? I'll sign it."

"It's in my car. But Jack, she doesn't want you to sign it. It offends her. All she hears when it's mentioned is that you might not be together forever. She can't bear that. She would never leave you."

"And I'm never going to leave her. I promised her forever and I meant it."

"She doesn't care about money, and honestly, I just want her to be happy. You make her happy, Jack. No one who knows you or has seen the two of you together thinks it matters."

"It matters to me. You asked me to take care of her. I gave you my word that I would, and that's what I'm trying to do. Please, just get it. She doesn't need to know about it."

"I don't keep things from Tess, especially not when they concern her," Omar said.

"I know, and normally I wouldn't ask. Please, help me do the right thing."

Omar nodded reluctantly and went to retrieve the document. When he returned, he handed it to Jack, who was waiting with a pen. He flipped to each page with a signature flag and signed it.

"Don't you think you should have a lawyer review that, or at least read it yourself?" Omar asked.

"I told you, I'm never going to leave her."

"Then why insist on signing it?" Omar asked.

"Because she deserves for the men in her life to protect her. I hope she stays with me forever, but it needs to be her choice." He shook his head and looked up. "It's funny, when we met and she told me she's a novelist, I assumed she was a struggling artist. When the time was right, I was going to ask her to move into my little apartment, so I could support her, take care of her."

Omar smiled. "She told me she would move into your place in a heartbeat. Material things have never mattered to Tess. You matter to her."

Jack looked back at the agreement and signed the last page. "Here," he said, handing it to Omar. "Please sign the witness line and see it gets to where it needs to go. Keep this between us."

Omar nodded. "It's not legally binding without her signature."

"Now she'll always be able to sign it, if she chooses."

"Do you know what she told me after your first weekend together? She said, 'He sees me, and I see him. I trust him completely, like I always did with you.' Then when you gave her that necklace, she FaceTimed me so I could see it. She was prattling on like a schoolgirl about how much she loves you, and then she said, 'He makes me feel like I'm enough, exactly as I am.' Tess has never felt that way before."

Jack smiled.

"I know you think you're lucky to be with her, but I want you to know that from the day I first met you, I knew she was also lucky to be with you. You're a good man. I'm thrilled you found each other."

Jack extended his hand. "Thank you. That means a lot to me."

Chapter 8

Their wedding day had finally arrived. Jack wore his finest black suit and waited in the living room with Joe and the justice of the peace.

Tess came out wearing a simple strapless white gown with a sweetheart neckline and her gold heart locket, her hair cascading in loose spiral curls, her lips stained pink. Jack covered his heart with his hands. "You are breathtaking. I can't wait to marry you."

She linked her arm to Omar's and walked to Jack, their eyes locked. "Be blissfully happy. I love you beyond measure," Omar whispered as he pecked her on the cheek and took her bouquet. The justice of the peace started the simple ceremony. Face-to-face and hand in hand, they recited the vows they had each written.

Jack looked at Tess with unadulterated adoration. "I've seen a lot of the bad in this world, and you are everything that's good. Since joining the military nearly twenty-five years ago, I've given a hundred percent of my loyalty and dedication to my job. Now I want to give that same level of commitment to you. I promise to love, honor, and protect you for all the days of my life. Tess, you are my world. I love you with my whole heart, forever."

A lone tear slid down Tess's face. Jack used his thumb to gently wipe it away. Tess smiled. "People often say that I have everything, but I've never had the one thing I truly longed for until I met you: happiness. There could be swarms of people around me, yet I so often felt a sense of loneliness. A deep, unending loneliness. Until you. Jack, you are the best thing that has ever happened to me. You are my joy, my strength, and my heart. You're my home and I'm yours. I love you with every fiber of my soul, and I always will."

"Together we are home," Jack whispered.

"Together we are home," Tess whispered in return, wiping away more tears.

Jack turned to the justice of the peace and said, "You better hurry up because I need to kiss her."

The justice of the peace smiled and said, "Jack, place a ring on Tess's finger as a symbol of your love and devotion."

Joe handed Jack the ring. He gently slipped the simple gold band on Tess's dainty finger.

"Now, Tess, place a ring on Jack's finger as a symbol of your love and devotion."

Omar handed her the ring. She slipped it on Jack's finger and gave his hand a little squeeze.

"I now pronounce you husband and wife," the justice of the peace declared. "You may kiss the bride."

Jack put his hand on the back of Tess's head and kissed her passionately as if no one were there. When he began to draw back, she pulled him back to her and they kissed again. Omar and Joe clapped and then each wiped wetness from their own eyes.

Jack turned to the justice of the peace and said, "Thank you."

"Yes, thank you so much," Tess added.

"My pleasure. I wish you a lifetime of wedded bliss. I'll see myself out."

Jack turned to their witnesses and shook each man's hand. Tess hugged Joe and then Omar. "You and Jack are perfect together. I wish you every happiness, Butterfly," Omar whispered. He then insisted on taking a few photographs of the newlyweds, despite the bride's complaints.

With Omar and Joe in charge of handling the incoming staff, Jack and Tess excused themselves to spend their first hours as a married couple alone. When they got to their bedroom door, Jack picked Tess up and carried her across the threshold. He carefully put her down and said, "I'm the luckiest person alive."

"That's exactly how I feel," she cooed.

After making love, they cuddled in bed, exchanging tender kisses. Tess sighed contentedly, burrowing into Jack.

"My wife, beautiful inside and out," he said, caressing her bare shoulder.

"I never thought I'd get married," she confessed, admiring her gold wedding band.

"Why not?"

"I believed so deeply in romantic love, but I had never fallen in love, not until you. At some point, I just assumed I never would. Maybe I wasn't ready for that kind of closeness and intimacy, for someone to really see me. I don't know." She shook her head. "All I do know is that everything changed when we met."

He placed a kiss on the tip of her nose. "Growing up, I always assumed I'd get married and start a family. That's all I knew from my upbringing, which was pretty traditional. Church and apple pie. But then, after the military, the path I took was so much darker than I ever could have imagined." He ran his hand through his hair. "From then on, I figured I'd be alone. It was safer that way."

"You didn't invite any relatives to our wedding. Do you keep in touch with your family?"

He shook his head. "I had to let them go a long time ago. My work was too dangerous. Family wasn't an option. I made peace with it, not only the things I had to do on the job but the personal sacrifices." She ran her finger down the side of his face. He kissed the tip of her nose again and continued, "But now I have you. Tess, you're everything to me."

"And you are to me." She paused to enjoy the moment. "The party is starting soon. So, what do I need to know about your guests?"

"It's just the folks from my group at work. They're all good people. There is this one guy, Chris, who's kind of a jerk. He wanted my job and resents me. Everyone else is cool. What about your friends?"

"Oh, it's sort of a random group. My publisher, Claire, my assistant, Crystal, and then a smattering of friends from all over. A hairstylist, an actress, a singer. I mainly want you to meet my friend Abdul and his wife. They came all the way from the Middle East to be here. Abdul is very special to me."

"Tell me about him," Jack said.

"I would rather let you meet him for yourself. But I will tell you that he is one of the people I respect most in this world. He's also one of the only people who I feel really understands me. He has a slow, considered way of speaking. I hang on to every wise word. I can't wait for you to meet."

"Then I can't wait to meet him."

Tess looked at the clock. "Honey, we'd better get dressed before our guests arrive."

"Just one more minute. I want to kiss my wife."

When they were finally able to tear themselves out of bed, Tess changed into a sleek black jumpsuit with a plunging neckline, and as always, her heart locket. Jack wore black slacks and a lightweight black sweater. They left their room just before eight, and as promised, Omar and Joe had taken care of everything. The bride and groom were ready to greet their guests.

Chapter 9

"Is that the actress from . . ." Bobby began to ask.

Jack nodded.

Bobby shook his head in amazement. "I think she won an Oscar last year."

"Wow, Tess has quite an impressive and diverse group of friends," Joe remarked. "Who's that woman she's speaking to?"

"A good friend from New York. They met waiting in line for a concert and hit it off," Jack replied.

Joe laughed. "She really is one of a kind."

Just then, Chris walked over and shook Jack's hand. "Congratulations. You've certainly done well for yourself."

Bobby rolled his eyes. Before Jack could respond, Tess flitted over. She kept one hand in her pocket and intertwined her other arm with Jack's.

"Sweetheart, this is Chris. We work together."

"A pleasure to meet you," Chris said.

"Likewise," Tess replied.

"I was just congratulating Jack. He certainly married up," Chris said.

"Huh. Isn't that funny? I thought I was the one who married up, being that Jack is an American hero and all."

A smile flashed across Joe's face.

"Well, I suppose at the end of the day, all women are the same anyway. Trust me, Jack, if she's anything like my wife, she'll be laying down house rules before you know it," Chris lamented.

"I only have one house rule, and since all women are alike, I'm sure it's the same rule your wife has," Tess said.

"What's that?" he asked.

"Morning sex. There should always be time for morning sex."

Chris's jaw dropped, along with everyone else's. Jack turned beet red, looked down, and chuckled.

Tess pecked him on the cheek. "Please excuse me, my love. I see that Abdul and Layla have arrived." She walked away, Chris's mouth still agape.

"Oh, you're a lucky man, Jack," Joe said with a laugh.

"Seriously, can you get her to talk to Gina?" Bobby added.

They all clinked their beer bottles.

"I'm gonna go get something to eat. Congrats again," Chris mumbled, slithering away.

As soon as Chris was out of earshot, Joe burst into laughter. "Tess is a pistol, Jack. She doesn't take any crap, and she had his number right away."

"She's seriously awesome," Bobby said. "I love her."

"Not as much as I do," Jack said.

Tess and Omar walked over with the older couple who had just arrived. "Honey, these are my special friends, Abdul and Layla. This is my husband, Jack, and these are our friends Joe and Bobby. They all work together."

"Very nice to meet you," Jack said, extending his hand.

"Are you exhausted from your trip?" Tess asked. "They flew in yesterday from Dubai to be here," she told the group.

"We are well rested," Layla replied. "Thank you for taking care of the arrangements for us. The flowers in the hotel are spectacular. I can't believe you remembered my favorites."

"It was the least I could do. I couldn't possibly get married without you and Abdul. It was so generous of you to come all this way."

"You're very kind," Abdul said. "We wouldn't have missed it for the world. Anything for you, Tess. You are my light."

Tess blushed. "You know the difficult job that Jack and his friends have. I wanted you to tell them about your work. It's the other side of the same coin. Like me, you see the world in terms of light and dark. I was hoping you could tell them about the light." She turned to the group. "Abdul is ambassador of the arts for the United Arab Emirates. For many years, he's been working to promote peace around the world through the arts."

"That's incredible," Joe said. "Is that how you two met?"

Tess nodded. "Omar told me about what Abdul was trying to achieve, and I simply had to meet him."

"When we met, we knew we were kindred spirits," Abdul explained. "I always felt that I saw people differently than others do. As a boy, I thought there was something wrong with me, but as I got older, my faith showed me that what I thought was a detriment was actually my path forward. It wasn't until I met Tess that I knew I wasn't alone. She's the first person I've met who sees people as I do, lasering in on their core humanity. Tess, do you agree?"

"Yes. It was such a relief. For years, I felt misunder-stood. People assumed that I must be childlike or naïve to see the world the way I do. They thought I couldn't see the differences between people, as if that were something to aspire to. But when you don't see people's differences, you don't see their humanity or their struggles. How could I write without truly witnessing people?" She paused and lowered her voice. "I see differences, details. But I also see something beyond them. I can hold two thoughts."

Abdul smiled. "Precisely."

"Please tell them about what you do," Tess said.

Abdul proceeded to tell the group about his work. They listened intently, their eyes growing wider as he went on. When he was finished, each one thanked him.

"I had no idea this was going on," Bobby said.

"Me either. Amazing work," Joe added.

Jack looked astounded. "I'm so impressed. It restores my faith."

"I told you. It's awe-inspiring. He's one of the most incredible human beings I've ever known," Tess said.

Abdul smiled modestly. "Tess has not shared her role in this effort."

"I've done nothing," Tess insisted. "This is about *your* work."

Abdul laughed and turned to Omar. "Do you think giving away millions of books is nothing? Do you think that what she has done for the women who read those books, many in secret, is nothing? Tell me, Omar, when she was standing by my side, touring the Middle East against everyone's advice, with all the horrific rape and death threats, refusing the extra security we all knew she needed, did you feel that was nothing? Perhaps my memory fails."

Omar's expression turned serious. "It was terrifying and very real. I begged her not to do it."

Tess looked down.

"Butterfly, it wasn't nothing," Omar said.

Jack, Joe, and Bobby couldn't look away, listening intently.

"Do you know what I remember, Abdul?" Tess said.

"Please tell me," he replied.

"How you taught me to transform myself into a vessel and shield myself in light for protection. I couldn't have survived those years without that skill. Thank you."

Abdul tilted his chin downward. "Knowing who you are in your soul, I always thought it must have been quite difficult for you. Not the people, but all the rest of it, the accolades, the attention, the chatter, as you would say. Tell me, was it difficult?"

"Difficult?" she whispered, a tear trickling down her face. "It was excruciating."

"Why did you do it?"

She wiped her cheek. "You already know the answer. There's only one reason to do anything."

He smiled. "For love."

She nodded.

Jack lightly rubbed her back, tracing his finger down her spine.

"That reminds me of the most harrowing day of our tour," Abdul said. "Do you remember?"

"Of course."

Abdul looked at the group. "There was a mob and no way past them. We were going to miss our next scheduled appearance. Our security team stuck us in a hotel room and told us we needed to cancel our next stop. Tess refused. She ordered them out of the room. You should have seen their faces; they were not used to a woman giving them commands. When they left, she looked me squarely in the eyes and said, 'The only way out is through.' I reluctantly agreed. Tess, do you remember what we did next?"

She smiled.

He took her hands, closed his eyes, and continued, "We held hands and quietly chanted, 'There is only darkness and light, and love is the bridge between them.' We repeated those words over and over again. 'There is only darkness and light, and love is the bridge between them.' We opened the door, and the guards asked what we were doing. I'll never forget, Tess said, 'We're leaving. You can come with us or stay here,' and she marched past them." He stopped to laugh.

"What happened next?" Joe asked.

"We passed safely through the crowd," Abdul said.

"Wow. That was very brave, Tess," Joe said.

Tess shook her head. "That's what Abdul thought at the time too. But now he knows better."

"What do you mean?" Jack asked.

"Not caring what happens to you is not the same as being brave."

Abdul smiled. "But tonight, Tess, I see a hint of something in your eyes I've never seen before: fear." He squeezed her hands. "It's wonderful. I'm very happy for you. You must finally feel like you have something to lose."

Two more guests walked through the front door, and Tess said, "Ah, it looks like I'm literally saved by the bell. My friend Mick is here, please excuse me."

She sauntered off. The group looked over to see who was arriving. Their jaws hit the floor. Bobby stammered, "Uh, is that . . ."

Jack shook his head in disbelief. "She said one of her friends was a singer."

Abdul smiled. "That's how she sees him. She sees something beyond the details."

✦ ✦ ✦

Tess and Mick ambled over to the group, another man trailing behind.

"Abdul and Layla went to get some food," Omar said. He shook Mick's hand. "Great to see you."

"You too, Omar. Tess called, so here I am," Mick replied. He leaned close to Tess with a mischievous glint in his eyes. "I'm just dying to meet the man who landed you, darling. It's rare I meet a man luckier than I am."

She giggled. "This is my husband, Jack."

"I've heard quite a bit about you. You've swept this one off her feet. A pleasure," Mick said, extending his hand.

"So amazing to meet you," Jack replied, shaking his hand.

"And these are our friends Bobby and Joe," Tess said.

"Nice to meet you," they said, starstruck.

"Oh, and this goon behind me is Eddie. They won't let me travel without personal security, an insurance thing," Mick groaned, rolling his eyes. "I brought what you asked for. Eddie's got it in that tube. Where should he put it?"

"Oh, thank you. He can stick it over there by the door," she said. "Can I get you something to drink?"

"I'll get it, and then we dance," he replied, squeezing her hand.

"The bar is set up through there, in the dining room."

"Sparkling water, no fruit for you?" he asked.

"Please."

"I'll be back."

As he walked off, Jack looked at her. "He knows what you drink?"

"Well of course, honey. Don't your friends know what you drink?"

He let out an audible huff and smiled.

"I feel like I'm having an out-of-body experience. You know I love their music," Bobby said.

"I remember," Tess replied.

"Butterfly, I see Clay chatting with Abdul and Layla. I'm going to join them unless you need me," Omar said.

"Go, enjoy yourself."

"But if Mick invites us to stay at his place in London again, you have to say yes. Pretty please?"

"I told you, never again."

"But why, Butterfly?"

"Because I'm not nocturnal."

"I know, but it was so much fun."

Tess shook her head. "You're impossible. Go spend time with your handsome man before he has second thoughts about you."

"That was cold, Tess," he said with a smirk.

Omar walked off as Mick returned with drinks. "So Jack, your job is fascinating. Tell me about saving the world," he said.

Jack laughed. They spoke until Mick's glass was empty. Mick looked at Tess devilishly and said, "Well, darling, shall we dance?"

"Sure," she replied. She rested a hand on Jack's chest. "We always dance."

Mick put his glass down. "But first, I must ask you something. Darling, is your husband a jealous man?"

"He knows he has no reason to be."

Jack blushed.

"Good," Mick said. "Because you know how I dance, and he looks like he could hurt me."

"Honey, my husband could snap your neck before that crossing guard you hired has time to get his hands off the cheese tray."

Jack nearly spit out his drink. Everyone held their laughter until Mick burst into hysterics. "Oh, darling, I've missed you." He hollered, "Eddie, get your grubby hands off the Brie!"

"Ha! That's the line of the night. It's even better than 'There's not enough meat on this deli platter.' They really should leave these things to the professionals," Tess said.

Mick laughed.

"You've seen *Spinal Tap*?" Bobby asked.

"Of course," Tess replied.

"What's *Spinal Tap*?" Jack asked.

"It's a mock documentary about a rock band. It's kind of the worst and best thing ever," Bobby said.

"Totally," Tess agreed. "And since you've never seen it, Jack, I know what we'll be doing tomorrow."

Mick took Tess's hand. "Shall we dance?"

"After you." She followed him, looked over her shoulder, and winked at Jack.

✦ ✦ ✦

Later in the evening, Tess was sitting in the corner chatting with Mick and her hairdresser, Denise. Mick got up and strolled over to Omar, Jack, Joe, and Bobby.

"That Denise is quite a girl," Mick said. "Tess always had the coolest friends. Jack, let's have some fun with your new bride. Omar, can you play a certain song?"

"Oh, I know what you're thinking. She'll be cross with me," Omar said.

Mick laughed. "Let's fill Jack and his friends in."

They listened eagerly.

"Tess threw a party several years ago in LA," Omar said. "She had a gorgeous yard, the whole thing illuminated with twinkly lights."

"And she was wearing this fabulous long, flowy white dress. It was impossibly LA," Mick added. "Anyway, Elton's 'Tiny Dancer' came on, and a few of us noticed Tess started to dance. She was actually twirling about like a ballerina. It was glorious. We loved watching her so much that we didn't want it to end. Someone had the idea to put it on repeat. Who was that?" Mick asked.

"It was Ronnie," Omar said.

"Yes! The rascal!" Mick exclaimed. "So, we put the song on repeat. Tess danced to it four or five times before she noticed. When she finally realized, she got so hysterical she collapsed into a heap on the grass. It was magnificent."

The men all belly laughed.

"Omar, go put it on," Mick directed.

Omar shook his head and said, "You're taking the heat for this one," before he headed off to change the music.

"It's the pre-chorus," Mick said. "I guarantee that she'll start moving, like she can't help it. Then when the chorus comes, *bang*."

Omar returned a moment later, just as the song began to play.

As if pulled by an invisible string, Tess stood up. "Here we go," Mick said.

Soon, Tess was twirling in the corner as if no one were there, as promised. Jack was beaming. Mick and Omar started cackling so loudly that it drew Tess's attention. Her mouth flew open, and she started shaking her head and laughing. She flipped them the middle finger and just continued dancing. They all laughed so hard they could hardly stand.

"High priestess of pain, my ass," Mick said. "That girl is a ray of light."

"What are you talking about?" Jack asked.

"Some asshole reviewer. He had her all wrong," Mick replied.

Omar sighed. "After her third novel came out, a reviewer wrote a story titled 'The People's High Priestess of Pain Is Back at It.' It gutted her. Everyone else called her inspirational and the book 'a breath of fresh air,' but that label stuck and it's all she remembered. It wasn't the review. She doesn't give a shit about that. It was what the words meant. She wears those words like a scarlet letter."

Jack turned his attention back to Tess, still dancing as if only she could hear the music.

At the end of the night, only a couple of their closest friends remained. As they were saying goodbye to Bobby and Gina, Tess grabbed the cardboard tube by the door.

"Here, Mick brought this for you," she said, handing it to Bobby.

"For me?" he asked in amazement.

"It's a poster signed by the whole band. One of their songs came on at the bar once, and you mentioned they were your favorite group."

"Are you serious? I don't know what to say. That's . . . unbelievable!" he stammered. He turned to Gina. "Oh my God, is this the coolest thing ever or what?" He turned back to Tess. "Thank you so much," he said, hugging her. "Congratulations again, you guys."

After they left, Omar said, "Okay, Tiny Dancer, that's a wrap."

"I'm gonna get you for that," she warned.

Omar smiled. "You two should get to bed. Clay and I will make sure the caterers finish the cleanup. We'll let ourselves out and lock up when everyone is gone."

Tess hugged him. "Thank you. I love you."

"I'm so happy for you, Butterfly."

"Thank you," Jack said, shaking his hand. "Good night, Clay."

"Oh, if you two didn't get any wedding cake, there's still some left," Omar said.

"Let's grab a piece," Jack said.

"I don't eat cake," Tess replied.

"Maybe you'll want a bite," he suggested.

On their way to the bedroom, they stopped in the dining room and picked up a piece of vanilla cake slathered in white frosting. When they got to their room at long last, Jack shut the door and Tess flicked off her shoes.

"Hey, come here, Mrs. Miller," he said.

"I like the sound of that."

He wove his fingers into her hair and kissed her. "Did you have fun tonight?"

"Oodles, but I couldn't wait to be alone with you. Did your friends have a good time?"

"Yeah. I think you made Bobby's whole life. That was really sweet."

"It was nothing."

Jack let out a puff and smiled. "You would say that."

She shrugged.

"I think the best part of the night was what you said to Chris. His mouth is probably still hanging open. I can't believe you said that."

"Actually, I thought I was quite reserved. I wanted to say blow jobs."

He laughed.

"That guy is kind of a prick," Tess said.

Jack smiled and picked up the piece of cake with his hand. "Would you like a taste, Mrs. Miller?"

She nodded and he held the cake up to her. She took a small bite, letting in the sweetness.

Chapter 10

In the early winter days after their wedding, Tess and Jack spent most of their time alone in their home oasis adjusting to married life and falling more in love with each passing moment.

One Saturday morning, Jack meandered into the kitchen to get some coffee when he saw Tess standing in front of the island with a tub of dried cranberries. He observed her making a small pile on a napkin, methodically counting each one. Without a word, he came up behind her, squeezed her waist, and dropped a kiss in her hair. She inhaled and leaned back onto his chest. He held her for a long moment before going to get his coffee.

After Tess finished preparing her snack, she turned to Jack and said, "Is it okay if I go upstairs to write?"

"Of course it is. Sweetheart, you don't have to ask me."

"It's just . . ."

"What, baby?"

"Well, you know I'm in the middle of a novel. When I get really immersed, sometimes I write for ten or twelve hours straight. Inspiration doesn't really care what day of the week it is, but now that I have you . . ."

"Hey," he said, taking her hand. "You can always do whatever you need to do."

She smiled. "It's just that I don't like missing time with you either."

He pecked her lips. "Good, then I won't be in your way if I go up to the office with you," he said, grabbing a mug of coffee, the newspaper, and his iPad.

A few hours later, Tess looked up from her laptop to see Jack sitting patiently in the corner wearing headphones and watching something on his iPad. They caught each other's eyes and smiled.

The day the first snow fell, Jack was in the kitchen unloading the dishwasher when Tess strolled into the room. She grabbed a container of granola and casually tossed a couple handfuls into a bowl, kissed Jack on the cheek, and headed to her office.

By the time the winter snow was beginning to melt, Tess and Jack were venturing out more. Jack became increasingly aware of just how famous Tess was, and in turn, he became hugely protective of her. He learned where to seat her in restaurants or bars so that she would have privacy, and he became attuned to the look in people's eyes when they recognized her. He could immediately tell by her demeanor whether to allow someone to approach her. There were times he wrestled with his desire to defend Tess and her disdain for violence.

One day, they were strolling through a museum when Jack noticed a couple of guys staring at Tess. She started pulling Jack in another direction, so he knew she wanted to steer clear. Sure enough, they quickly approached Tess, one of them saying, "Aren't you that writer? You're worth like a billion dollars."

Tess held Jack's hand, keeping her other hand snug in her pocket. She smiled at them and tried to walk away.

The guy hollered, "You don't have to be a bitch!"

Jack spun around, his face red. "What did you say?" he yelled.

"Jack, please, just ignore them. Please," Tess begged.

He looked at the guys and in an eerily calm voice said, "Don't ever speak to a woman that way."

They walked away.

"Thank you for not escalating it," Tess said.

"I wanted to thrash him," Jack replied.

"If you do that every time some jerk says something to me, it's going to be a very long and very violent life. It's okay to let it go, baby. Jack . . ."

"Yeah?"

They stopped walking, and she looked him in the eyes. "I would never want you to harm someone else for my sake. The only darkness that frightens me is in you."

He was stunned. "You're not scared of me?"

"Of course not. But sometimes I'm scared *for* you. It's your soul I care about, not guys like that."

Another night a few weeks later, Tess and Gina had plans to meet Jack and Bobby at a bar after work. The women arrived first. When Jack and Bobby walked in, two men were hassling them. "We told you, no thank you," Gina said to one of the guys, turning away from him. The other guy touched Tess's shoulder, and Jack and Bobby tore across the room.

Jack grabbed the guy's shoulders and screamed, "Don't touch her or you'll have to deal with me!"

"Get the fuck out of here. Now!" Bobby yelled.

When they sat down at the table, Tess looked at Jack. "You know, men try to pick up women sometimes. You might have overreacted."

"He touched you. I wanted to slam his head into the bar," Jack said.

"Well then, I guess your reaction wasn't that bad," she joked.

He looked upset and a little embarrassed. She brushed the side of his face. "It's okay. Just try to take a beat."

The scariest incident of all happened just as the trees were popping with light green buds. It was a Friday night at Shelby's Bar, and Tess, Jack, Joe, and Bobby were sitting at their usual table having a drink. Gina was at home with a cold, Clay was on call at the hospital, and Omar was running late. A tall man in a black suit walked into the bar. Tess clenched Jack's hand and muttered, "I don't believe it."

"What is it?" he asked.

"I hope that man doesn't come over here," she replied.

"Who is he?" Jack asked.

"Arlo Mathers. He's a publisher. Let's just say he has very poor manners with women."

"We've got you," Bobby said.

Joe nodded. "Absolutely."

Arlo moseyed up to the table. "Tess Lee, I can't believe it." Tess didn't respond.

"I'm in town for a conference and stopped for a drink," he added.

"Congratulations," Tess replied briskly.

He snorted. "Tess, may I please speak with you privately? I'd love to clear the air."

"I have nothing to say to you. Please leave. In fact, go get a drink somewhere else."

"But Tess, I . . ."

Jack stood up. "She asked you to leave."

Arlo snorted again. "Tess, you never looked better," he said, walking away from the table and out the door.

Jack sat down and draped his arm around Tess. "You okay, baby?"

She nodded. "Thank you for getting rid of him. Let's talk about something else."

Bobby started talking about all of Gina's plans for their wedding. Inspired by Tess and Jack's happiness, Bobby had finally proposed, and now his weekends consisted of meetings with photographers and florists.

Half an hour later, Omar arrived. "I'm so sorry I'm late. Butterfly, Larry is about to board his jet for Tokyo, and there are some questions about the giving statement in the end credits. It would be fastest if you just called him. Pretty please?"

"Sure thing. Excuse me, gentlemen. I'll be right back."

As Tess walked out, Omar raised his hand, signaling the waitress for a beer. He grabbed a handful of pretzels and started gobbling them. "Insane day, I can't remember when I last ate something."

"Omar, who's Arlo Mathers?" Jack asked.

"Well, that's a name I hoped to never hear again. He's in publishing. Reprehensible guy. Tess had a bad feeling about him from the moment they met. Her instincts are always spot-on," Omar replied. The waitress delivered his beer, and he took a swig.

"Tess said he has poor manners with women," Jack said.

"Ha! That's like saying Charles Manson is impolite. Another good thing that came from getting her out of LA is that she's far away from that sexual predator. I'm telling you, he was obsessed. I still don't understand how he managed to lure her out of that charity soirée. Thank God those men found her in time. It took both of them to pull him off her. She should have pressed charges; she had bruises on her wrists for weeks. But you know how she is, never thinks of herself, didn't want to risk harming the charity. Why are we talking about this asshole?"

Jack started shaking with rage. "He was here tonight. He came up to the table and asked Tess to speak with him."

"Arlo Mathers was here?" Omar said. His face fell. "I just asked Tess to go outside by herself."

Jack leapt from the table, the three other men following close behind. They raced outside. Tess was leaning against the building with Arlo standing in front of her, his arm against the brick exterior, blocking her in. Jack flew over, grabbed him, and punched him. He fell to the ground, blood spewing from his broken nose. Jack leaned down for another go at him, but Bobby grabbed him from behind.

"He isn't worth it," Bobby urged. "Do you really want Tess to see this?"

Jack stood over him, his chest heaving. Then he glanced back at Tess, hunched over, her face in her hands. He took a deep breath and went to her. "It's okay, baby. You're okay." He took her in his arms and rubbed her head. "Why didn't you tell me?"

"Because I love you more than I hate him."

Tess was equally protective of Jack. If someone would give him grief, in turn, Tess would give them hell. One spring day, they decided to have a picnic lunch at the park to enjoy the cherry blossoms bursting on the trees. Tess arrived at

Jack's office with a basket filled with homemade goodies. He was sitting in his office with Joe and Chris, deep in concentration, but broke into a huge smile when she appeared in his doorway. "Hi, sweetheart."

She greeted Joe and Chris and then turned to Jack. "I can wait outside while you finish up, honey."

"Jack, are you going somewhere?" Chris asked.

"Tess and I are stepping out for lunch. We can wrap this up when I get back," he replied.

Chris turned to Tess. "Do you really think it's responsible for Jack to leave in the middle of the day?"

Joe looked down and shook his head.

Jack opened his mouth to speak, but Tess jumped in. She stared Chris down and said, "I realize our national security might require the total sacrifice of a few soulless robots, and for this, the citizens of our country thank you. However, you might want to spend some quality time with your wife before you have the gall to insinuate that my husband is irresponsible." Then she flitted over to Joe, pecked him on the cheek, and said, "Always a pleasure to see you." She turned to Jack. "I'll be right outside, honey."

When she left the room, Joe burst into laughter. Jack shook his head, trying not to laugh.

"Tess really doesn't like me," Chris muttered.

"It's a real mystery," Joe said, wiping the tears from his eyes.

Jack chuckled.

Sometimes the stakes were higher. Tess hated how hard Jack was on himself. When he was dealing with a national security crisis or some terrorist threat, he would come home at all hours of the night, his eyes glazed from having faced the worst of humanity. Tess would curl up beside him, silently running her fingers along his body until she could feel him let the darkness go.

One late spring day, there was a suicide bombing in DC with several civilian casualties. Tess had spoken on the phone with Jack amidst the chaos, and he said, "It's my fault. I couldn't stop them in time." Tess waited in the living room until he finally came home at four in the morning. He headed straight to her. She stood up and looked into his haunted eyes, the weight of the world etched on his face. She brushed his cheek with the back of her hand, slipped her hand under the hem of his shirt, and slowly helped him pull it off. He started pulling off her clothes as she helped him out of the rest of his. She kissed him softly and guided him to the couch.

After making love, they held each other and she whispered, "It isn't your fault. You did everything you could."

He kissed the side of her head. "I couldn't wait to get home to you."

"Come on, let's grab the leftover Chinese food. We can curl up with this throw blanket and eat it cold out of the containers."

The hint of a smile crept onto his face. He pecked her again and said, "Okay, baby."

✦ ✦ ✦

Tess helped Jack in other ways too. One hot summer day, they were strolling through the park when a few little girls skipped past them holding popsicles that were melting down their arms. As he typically did, Jack lowered his head ever so slightly. Tess intertwined her fingers with his, pulled him close, and whispered, "The only way out is through. Just feel it." He took a breath and wiped tears from his eyes.

"Come here, baby," Tess said, leading him to a bench. They sat down, cozied up together, and she gently said, "Tell me more about Gracie."

"She loved flowers, especially purple ones."

The next morning over breakfast, Jack was reading the Sunday newspaper. He flipped past the comics and said, "Gracie loved comics."

Tess smiled. It was the first time he had ever mentioned Gracie on his own.

As much as Tess and Jack loved being together more with each passing day, they also enjoyed spending time with their friends. They had become a close-knit group and spent many evenings together, laughing uproariously. One crisp autumn night at the bar, they were sharing their most embarrassing and entertaining stories. Bobby told them a hilarious story from his time in the academy. When they all settled down, Jack nudged Tess. "Your turn."

"Hmm. I don't know," she replied.

"Oh, I do," Omar said gleefully. "Jack, you're going to love this. We were at a gala in London where Tess was being honored—"

"I know where this is going, and you're not telling that story," Tess interrupted, picking up a pretzel and flinging it at his head.

"Butterfly, I'll wear that basket as a hat, but I am telling the story," he said, grinning like a Cheshire cat.

"Fine, but I'm making two objections. First, I wasn't embarrassed."

"I know, but you should have been," Omar said, chucking a pretzel back at her. "But that's all right, I was embarrassed enough for the both of us."

She shook her head. "Second, it's not that funny."

"If by 'not that funny,' you mean it's epically funny, then you'd be right," he said with a chuckle. "In fact, it may be the funniest thing to ever happen to anyone."

She tossed another pretzel at him, but he dodged it.

"This must be good," Bobby said.

"Go on, Omar," Joe urged.

"You're all terrible," Tess protested, looking to Jack for support.

"Don't look at me, I want to hear it," Jack said.

She rolled her eyes. "Fine, but my objections stand." She crossed her arms and put on an exaggerated pout.

"Duly noted, Butterfly. So, Tess was in London, receiving an award for her humanitarian efforts in the arts."

"Such a ridiculous thing to receive an award for. People shouldn't be praised simply for being decent," Tess interjected.

"Nice attempt at deflection, Butterfly. You can give us a diatribe about the absurdity of awards another time," Omar said.

Tess rolled her eyes.

"Another of the honorees was—"

"Don't you say his name," Tess warned.

"Let's just say he was in the greatest band of all time."

Bobby's eyebrows arched sky-high. "You don't mean . . ."

"Yes, Paul himself," Omar replied. "Anyway, after the award ceremony, Paul was hosting a little party at his place and invited us. He had just purchased a Picasso at auction for something crazy like thirty million dollars, and he wanted Tess's opinion. You have to remember that she had just been honored as a literary genius and artistic visionary. So, Paul and all his guests stood around waiting to hear her profound words of wisdom. What does Tess do? She looks at the painting, cocks her head, and says, 'Peekaboo, why so blue?'"

They all cracked up.

"You did *not* say that!" Jack said through fits of laughter.

"I did," Tess replied, turning red.

"'Peekaboo, why so blue?' What does that even mean?" Bobby asked.

Tess shrugged. "I have no idea; it's just what came out. The whole situation was so absurd."

"What did Paul do?" Joe asked.

"Well, that's the best part of the story. At first, everyone just stood there in a state of shock. After a moment passed, Paul said, 'Too right, Tess. Peekaboo, why so blue?' as if she was some kind of genius. Everyone started clapping over this supposedly great insight," Omar said.

Everyone laughed uncontrollably, practically falling off their chairs.

"I still don't think it's that funny," Tess protested.

Try as he might, Jack was unable to stop laughing.

Omar finally composed himself. "Now, every time Paul wants to buy a piece of art, I mean even a bloody poster for his bathroom, he FaceTimes Tess to get her opinion."

They all laughed so hard they were holding their stomachs.

"He FaceTimes you?" Jack asked when he could get the words out.

"Not often," Tess replied.

"When was the last time?" Omar asked.

"About four months ago."

Omar raised his eyebrows. "And what did he want?"

Tess looked down sheepishly. "He was trying to choose between two Tiffany lamps, and he wanted my opinion."

Everyone laughed so hysterically they could hardly breathe. Even Tess was laughing now.

"She's like his art oracle," Omar squealed.

Jack pulled Tess to him. "You're supposed to be on my side," she said. "It's not that funny."

"I'm always on your side, but sweetheart, it *is* that funny."

✦ ✦ ✦

More than anything, Tess and Jack simply loved being alone together in their home. Together they felt like they inhabited their own private snow globe of light, safe from everything swirling outside. One Sunday morning, they woke up and quietly snuggled together before slipping out of bed, changing into running clothes, and going for a long jog to admire the colorful autumn leaves, as they had done in the days before. They bounded into their house dripping with sweat. Jack grabbed a water bottle and tossed one to Tess, and they both had a good drink before meandering to their shower.

As the water beat down, they started kissing and running their hands along each other's bodies. Jack slowly turned Tess in his arms, and she put her hands on the wall. He slid inside of her, and they made love. His body trembling, he kissed her shoulder. She turned toward him, and they stared into each other's eyes for a long moment before Jack turned off the faucet.

They dried off, got dressed, and meandered to the kitchen. Jack put on the coffee while Tess made oatmeal. She ladled out portions in two bowls and then grabbed some blackberries, casually sprinkling them on top of each serving. Jack came up behind her, squeezed her waist, and dropped a kiss in her hair. They headed to the living room with their breakfast to watch a morning news show. When they were done eating, they curled up on the couch together.

Tess stroked Jack's arm and he softly said, "That feels nice."

"I love being cozy together."

"Would you like to watch the game?"

"Sure," she replied.

Those were the first words they had spoken that day.

Through all these moments, Tess and Jack's bond grew. Soon the days had turned into a year. By the time the trees were shedding their last leaves, Tess had released her new novel, which she loved writing but declined to promote. At Jack's suggestion, she signed ten thousand copies for her publisher, giving fans a chance to buy autographed copies. Jack learned to look to Tess in his dark or dour moments, take a beat, and breathe. With her help, he found ways to let the darkness go. Friday nights with their friends grew into a series of game nights and potlucks at each other's homes, in addition to evenings at Shelby's Bar. And at total ease with one another, their home remained a safe harbor.

Chapter 11

When Jack's alarm went off that Wednesday morning, Tess jumped up. "Let me run in to brush my teeth."

He yawned and stretched his arms.

Soon, Tess returned to the bedroom wearing a black lace teddy. She sashayed to Jack's side of the bed. "Good morning, Mr. Miller."

He reached out and caressed her leg. "What's going on here? I have work, baby. You're going to make me late again."

"I'm simply enforcing the house code. You can be ten minutes late."

"Okay, wait for me," he said with a smile, and darted to the bathroom.

When he returned, Tess was kneeling at the edge of the bed. He walked over, ran his hands through her hair, and started kissing her. He paused long enough to say, "I can be twenty minutes late."

After making love, they lay in bed touching each other's faces. Jack said, "You know, I think I owe Chris one. If he hadn't been such a prick at our wedding, you may not have created such a great house rule. We have the best mornings."

She giggled. "We do. And the best nights."

He kissed her. "I'm so late."

"I know. Go get ready. I'll make you a coffee to go."

"Thank you," he said, kissing her one more time before slipping out of bed.

Fifteen minutes later, Jack whizzed into the kitchen, clean and dressed. "That was record timing. Here," Tess said, handing him a to-go tumbler and something wrapped in foil. "I fixed you coffee and a bagel."

"Thank you, sweetheart."

"I'm going to the library today to do research for my book. I'll stop at the store afterward to pick up something for dinner. Any special requests?"

"Whatever you want," he replied. He leaned in for a quick peck. "I love you."

"I love you too. Have a great day," she said, smiling widely.

Just past noon, Jack was reviewing a file with Joe when his cell phone rang.

"Miller here," he answered.

"Mr. Miller, this is Vivian, your house cleaner."

"Yes?"

"Something is wrong with Mrs. Miller, and I think you should come home right away."

"What happened?" he asked, panic in his voice.

"I don't know. When I arrived at your home, her phone was smashed in the kitchen and she was sitting in the living room. I could see something was terribly wrong. She said she wasn't safe, and then she ran and hid in the bedroom closet. She's in there now."

"Please don't leave her. I'm on my way," he said. He sprang up and raced out of the room.

Joe called after him. "What's going on?"

"Something happened to Tess!" he screamed.

He flew out of the parking garage, speeding toward their house and honking for other cars to move out of the way as he zoomed through every red light. He called Omar on the way.

"Hello?"

"It's Jack. Something's wrong with Tess. The cleaner called and said she's hiding in a closet. I'm on my way now."

"I'll meet you there," Omar said.

When Jack arrived at the house, he surveyed the scene: Tess's destroyed phone was on the kitchen counter, there was an open bottle of vodka and several packs of cigarettes strewn on the coffee table, and the house stank of stale smoke. He dashed into the bedroom. Vivian was standing at the closet door. "Move," he commanded.

Tess was curled up in a ball, cowering in the corner, her hair covering her face. He slid on the floor in front of her. "Tess, it's okay. I'm here," he said tenderly, reaching out to touch her.

She flinched and tried to pull herself further into the corner.

"Sweetheart, it's Jack. It's your Jack," he said.

Her head remained lowered, her arms clenched against her chest.

He reached his hand out and gently touched her shoulder, but she jerked away.

"Okay, it's okay. You just sit there for a minute," he said.

He slowly got up and stepped out of the closet. He looked at Vivian. "Tell me everything that happened from the second you got here."

"I let myself in like always. I noticed her broken phone right away. I saw she was sitting on the couch in the living room, which startled me because she's usually out or upstairs in her office. I apologized for barging in, but she didn't respond, so I walked over. She was smoking, which I've never seen her do before. She was trembling and wouldn't look at me, so I bent down and said, 'Ms. Lee, is everything all right?' She quietly said, 'Mrs. Miller. My name is Mrs. Miller.' I said, 'I'm sorry. Mrs. Miller, is there something I can do to help you?' She stared blankly ahead and just kept repeating, 'I'm not safe. I'm not safe.' Then she ran to the bedroom, got in the closet, and started mumbling, 'I'm not safe,' again. Eventually, she stopped talking altogether. I told her I was going to call you, and she didn't respond. She's been like this ever since."

Just then, Omar entered the bedroom. "Jack, what's going on?" he asked, his face flushed.

Jack pointed to the closet. Omar peeked in.

"What happened?"

"I don't know," Jack said, gripping his head with his hands.

"It's okay. We'll take care of her," Omar said. Then he gestured to Vivian. "Did she tell you what she knows?"

"Yeah."

"Thank you, Vivian. I think it would be best if you leave now," Omar said.

Vivian nodded and left.

Omar put his hand on Jack's shoulder. "I need you to stay calm and tell me everything that happened today. Don't leave anything out."

Jack took a breath and steadied himself. "We had sex this morning."

"And she was all right?" Omar asked.

Jack's eyes started to tear. "Yes, she was perfect. Then I got ready for work as she fixed me breakfast to take with me. Before I left, she was talking about going to the library and she asked what I wanted for dinner. She was so happy."

"Go on," Omar encouraged.

"The cleaner called just after noon. I raced home and found Tess's phone smashed in the kitchen, and Tess was like this. She'd been drinking, Omar."

"It's okay. She's not an alcoholic; that's not why she doesn't drink. What did Vivian say?"

"She said Tess was sitting on the couch, trembling. Vivian asked if she could help her. She called her Ms. Lee, and Tess said her name was Mrs. Miller. Then she said she wasn't safe and came in here. She repeated that she wasn't safe for a little while and then stopped. I tried to tell her I was here and to comfort her, but she wouldn't even let me touch her. She recoiled when I tried," he said, now getting hysterical. "I haven't even seen her face. I don't know if someone hurt her. Omar, please help her."

Omar nodded and slowly stepped into the closet. He sat on the floor in front of Tess. "Butterfly, it's me, Omar. You're safe now. Jack and I are both here. Everything is okay. I need to know if you understand me. Jack said you don't want anyone to touch you. That's fine. But I need you to look at me so I know that you understand what I'm saying. Can you do that, Butterfly? Can you please look at me?" He waited patiently for a moment, and Tess raised her head and looked at him. Omar smiled. "Thank you. Now let's get you somewhere more comfortable. Do you want to lie down in your bed?" She shook her head so slightly it was almost imperceptible. "That's okay. Do you want to go have a seat on the couch, where you were earlier?" She nodded faintly. Omar said, "I'm going to get up now. You can follow me." He stood up slowly and walked out of the closet. He gestured for Jack to step back. Omar peeked into the closet. "Are you ready?" Tess stood up, her shoulders slumped. She shambled to the living room behind Omar and sat down on the couch.

"Jack, please get her a glass of water."

Omar sat on the chair adjacent to Tess, observing. On the coffee table were a couple packs of cigarettes, a plate with several butts, and an open vodka bottle missing a couple of shots. Tess reached for a cigarette and the lighter. She lit the cigarette with shaking hands, exhaling lines of smoke. Jack returned with the water. Omar placed the glass in front of Tess.

"Try to take a few sips of water, please," he said. "I'm going to speak with Jack for a minute. We'll be right in the kitchen if you need us."

Tess continued puffing on her cigarette.

Omar and Jack huddled in the kitchen.

"Have you ever seen her like this before?" Jack asked.

"No, never. This is what I think: There are no signs that anyone physically hurt her today. I think she received a phone call from someone who has hurt her or someone she's terrified will hurt her. She's not a fearful person, so it's something real."

"That Arlo guy?" Jack asked.

"I doubt it. Tess isn't scared of him and this runs deeper," Omar replied.

"The men who assaulted her when she was a girl?"

"They're both dead, Jack. But I think whoever called has wounded her deeply, and now she's having a significant post-traumatic stress response. We need to find out where her last call came from."

"Her phone is shattered. I'll call Bobby. He can find out."

"In the meantime, I need you to try to see the positive here."

Jack let out a small noise. "There's something positive?"

"Yes. What we are witnessing takes tremendous strength. When this happened, her first reaction was to numb herself; that's why she's drinking and smoking. It wasn't enough to block out the trauma, so she's gone into this protective state.

She's retreated inward to keep herself safe. She's protecting herself from something so painful or frightening that she isn't yet able to deal with it. Jack, she didn't try to hurt herself. I believe she's trying to heal herself. She's responsive when I speak to her and in control of her body, and those are good things."

"She won't let me touch her," Jack said, his eyes welling with tears. "She flinched when I tried. She won't even look at me."

"It's because she loves you more than anything. You can see straight through her. She needs to hide right now, and she can't do that with you. Believe me, when she's ready, you'll be the one she looks for. I'm certain."

Jack sniffled. "How can we help her?"

"For a number of reasons, I think the best thing we can do is to try to deal with it here in her home. I'm trained for this and I know her. I can do this, but you should be prepared for her to be like this for many hours or days. I need to know if you're up for it."

"Yes. What do we do?"

"The idea is to let her choose to come back to us, not to force her. She's a sexual assault survivor and it's clear she doesn't want to be touched, so we should honor that. She needs personal space. You should stay nearby, because it will bring her comfort, but you shouldn't try to force her to look at you. We should speak in quiet tones, nothing jarring. Also, and please don't be alarmed, but I don't want her alone other than to use the bathroom, and even then, you should stand right outside the door. We need to get rid of anything she could use to harm herself: razors, scissors, knives, pills. If you have a gun, secure it."

Jack looked down, his breath labored.

"It's just a precaution. Even after everything that's happened to her in her life, she's never tried to hurt herself, including today. We just need to be careful."

Jack nodded. "What about the cigarettes and vodka?"

"Leave them. They're comforting her, and I don't want to take that away. I'm going to call Clay and ask him to drop off some clothes and a toothbrush later tonight. I'll stay here as long as it takes, until she's a hundred percent back to her normal self and we've dealt with whatever or whoever caused this."

"Thank you," Jack said. "I'm so grateful we have you, Omar. I wouldn't know what to do."

"I promise, I will get you both through this. Do you have ibuprofen or something? She's been drinking, and most likely on an empty stomach. I want to try to get her to take something so she doesn't end up with a terrible headache."

"Above the kitchen sink."

"I'll try to get her to take them, and then I'll see if I can convince her to eat something. While I'm doing that, you can go put all those items we discussed out of reach. You might as well change into something more comfortable too."

Jack nodded and set off.

Omar retrieved ibuprofen for Tess and sat down in the chair near her. "Please take these and a good drink of water or you'll get a bad headache, Butterfly," he said, placing the pills beside her glass.

She picked up the pills and swallowed them, taking several sips from her glass. Then she lay down on the couch, flat on her back, staring at the ceiling. Jack returned ten minutes later in sweatpants and a T-shirt. "It's taken care of, and I made a couple of phone calls," he said.

"I think Tess wants to rest. Where can I find a blanket for her?" Omar asked.

"The upstairs hall closet," Jack replied.

Omar got up and Jack sat in the chair on the other side of the room, where he had a clear view of Tess's face. The distress was gone from her eyes, but now they were completely vacant. When Omar returned, he held the blanket in front of Tess. "Do you want this?"

She took the blanket, unfurled it over her body, turned to the inside of the couch, and shut her eyes. Jack and Omar stayed with Tess while she slept.

When she finally woke from her nap four hours later, she got up and ambled toward their bedroom without a word. Jack followed her. She walked into the bathroom, shutting the door behind her. He stood on the other side of the door, counting the seconds, terrified of her being out of sight. He heard the toilet flush and the faucet turn on and off. A moment later, she opened the door and returned to the living room couch.

Omar came into the room holding a dish with scrambled eggs, which he placed on the coffee table with silverware. "Tess, please try to eat," he said.

She didn't touch the eggs and instead reached for a cigarette. After finishing her smoke, she lay down, again staring at the ceiling.

Jack's cell phone rang, and he walked into the kitchen to take the call. He returned a couple minutes later and motioned for Omar.

"That was Bobby. Her last phone call came from a public phone in a hospital in Rhode Island. There's no way to know who made the call. Do you have any ideas?"

"Nothing comes to mind," Omar replied. "I'm sorry. I don't know how to make sense of it."

Jack couldn't hide the disappointment on his face. "We should be near Tess."

They sat in the living room until Clay dropped off a bag for Omar at eleven o'clock that night, and he settled into one of the guest rooms after advising Jack to wake him immediately if anything changed. Tess lay awake all night, just looking at the ceiling. Jack sat in the chair watching her.

✦ ✦ ✦

Omar emerged just after dawn and came to check on them. "Good morning, Butterfly," he said with a sweet smile, and then he walked into the kitchen with Jack following behind. "No change?" he asked.

"She's been like that all night," Jack replied, his forehead creased with worry.

"Did you get any sleep?"

Jack shook his head. "You?"

"Barely. I'm trying to keep it together to get you both through this, but it's torture seeing her like this. Let's have a shift change. Go take a shower."

"I don't want to leave her," Jack said.

"I'll sit with her. It won't do her any good if you're a mess when she needs you. Take a shower and shave. Then I want her to shower and brush her teeth. She needs to have some sense of routine. You can set out a towel and some fresh clothes for her. We need to give her privacy, but I also don't want her unsupervised. Leave the bathroom door ajar while she showers and stand outside of it. Don't look and don't speak to her unless she asks for you. Once she's done, I'll try to get her to eat some breakfast. Getting something solid into her would help her chemistry enormously. Okay?"

Jack nodded. "Yeah, okay."

He returned fifteen minutes later, looking less disheveled but still deeply troubled and exhausted. Tess was sitting up on the couch.

"Butterfly, you need to brush your teeth and take a shower. Please get up and go. Jack will make sure you have everything you need."

She didn't move.

"Butterfly, you'll feel better if you shower and change into fresh pajamas. Please."

She got up and shuffled to the bathroom, Jack following behind. He pointed to a folded towel on the counter and fresh clothes beside it. "Those are for you. There's one of those hair scrunchie things on top; I know sometimes you don't like to get your hair wet in the shower." He turned on the shower and tested the temperature until it was just right. "Sweetheart, I'll be right outside the door if you need anything."

He left the room and leaned against the wall just outside the door, desperately trying to hold it together. Tess brushed her teeth and showered. When she was done, she opened the bathroom door and Jack stepped aside. She walked into the kitchen where Omar was waiting.

"I made you coffee, juice, and oatmeal. Please take a seat," he said, pulling out a barstool.

She sat down and picked up the coffee. She took a sip and then slid off the stool and returned to the couch. She lit a cigarette and slowly drank the coffee. Omar brought the juice and oatmeal to her. "Please try to have a little, Butterfly. You need something in your stomach." She didn't touch them. When she was done with the coffee, she put the mug down and lay on her back, shutting her eyes.

Jack walked calmly to the kitchen, and when he was out of Tess's sight, he started crying, holding his head and rocking back and forth. Omar came and put his hands on Jack's shoulders. "I know it's difficult. It's killing me too, more than you know. I promise you that she will be okay. She won't be like this forever."

"When my daughter was sick, when she died, I felt so powerless. I never thought I could feel that helpless again. And now this is happening to Tess, my Tess," he sobbed. "I can't lose her. She's everything to me. I feel so useless. I would do anything to make everything all right."

Omar rubbed his back. "You are. You are doing more than you know."

Jack straightened up, wiped his face, and caught his breath. "We shouldn't leave her alone."

A couple of hours later, Omar tried to get Tess to eat something, but she refused again. In the afternoon, he had an idea and motioned to Jack.

"Do you think you could get Bobby to come over here?" Omar asked.

"Yes. He and Joe have both been texting and offering to come help, but I didn't think we should let anyone near her."

"She must be starving and dehydrated. At this point, food is what would help her the most, but it's not something we can force. Neither of us is able to get her to eat, so I think we need to get someone else in here with lighter energy to try. Bobby has the right demeanor, and she really likes him."

"I'll call him," Jack said.

"Okay. I'll let him know exactly what to do."

An hour later, Bobby arrived holding two plastic bags.

"Thanks for coming," Jack said.

"Of course. Anything for you and Tess. How's she doing?"

Jack's expression was pained. "She hasn't spoken or eaten in thirty hours. She's lying on the couch."

Bobby glanced over. "I'm so sorry. Hopefully, this will help. Here, I picked up some sandwiches for you guys. I figured you could use something to eat. How are you holding up, Jack?"

"I'm a wreck. Just please try to get her to eat."

"Omar, is there anything I should know that you didn't tell me over the phone?" Bobby asked.

"Try to talk to her normally. She'll be unresponsive, but talk anyway. She feels comfortable with you, so be yourself. Don't touch her or get too close. Keep it light and easy," Omar said.

"Got it."

Bobby walked into the living room. "Hey, Tess. I brought some food," he said casually, placing the bag on the coffee table.

She rolled onto her side to face him. He opened the bag and took out two bottles of water, two tubs of soup, and a box of crackers. He opened the waters and placed one in front of her. Then he took napkins, plastic spoons, and a paper plate out of the bag. "I got us tomato soup. It's always been one of my favorites, and Omar told me that's what you like," he said, removing the lid from her container. "It might be hot, though, so we should let it cool off." Then he put the paper plate in the middle of the table, opened the box of crackers, and spilled some onto the plate. "Jack said these are your favorites. The box says they're made with cassava. I have no idea what that is, but it sounds healthy. Gina's always trying to get me to eat healthier. She says I can't live on burgers and chicken wings."

Tess sat up, facing him, her legs curled up in front of her body.

Jack and Omar were standing in the kitchen with bated breath.

"Anyway, I'm curious to try these," Bobby said, picking up a few crackers. He popped one in his mouth. "Hey, you're right. These are really good. Want some?" he asked, pushing the paper plate closer to her.

She reached over, picked up a cracker, and ate it.

"I dig 'em," Bobby said, picking up a handful and eating them one by one. "Anyway, the thing is that I'm not really a good cook. It makes it a lot harder to eat healthy."

Tess reached over and picked up a handful of crackers, sat back, and ate them slowly as he spoke.

Omar put his hand on Jack's shoulder and whispered, "He's so good. I knew this would work."

Jack nodded and sniffled, tears in his eyes.

"Gina is a pretty good cook, but she's always busy, so we end up getting a lot of takeout. Jack told me you're a great cook, but he did tell me a funny story about a time you made him muffins. He said you forgot an ingredient or something and they didn't rise. He said they were like hockey pucks, but you were so disappointed and he felt so bad for you that he ate them anyway. Jack's always doing things like that. He's such a good guy, and he loves you so much."

Tess finished her crackers and took a few sips of water.

"You know, the soup is probably cool enough by now," Bobby said, picking up his container. He ate a spoonful. "Mmm, this is really good."

Tess picked up her soup and began eating. Jack had to turn away, tears streaming down his face.

"You know, since you're the one who helped me pick out Gina's engagement ring, I have to confess that I'm a little nervous. Don't get me wrong, I know she's the one. I can't wait to marry her. But I'm a little worried about living together. I've never lived with anyone before, and I don't want to get on her nerves. Jack told me that you two have never had a fight. I told him I didn't understand how two people could live together for a year and never argue. He told me you said there's no reason to ever argue because you love each other and everything else is just details to sort out. I thought that was really beautiful. I hope Gina and I can be like that."

They both continued eating.

"After I proposed, Gina said she hopes we can be half as happy as you and Jack. Everyone feels that way. What you two have is so special. Jack hasn't been the same since he met you, in the best way. I used to feel kind of bad for him. I mean, he's the nicest, most honorable, loyal guy in the world, and he gave everything to serve his country, and I always felt bad that he didn't really have a life beyond that.

You gave him a life. You mean everything to him. I'm sure you know that, but I just wanted to tell you. Anyway, we're going to start looking at apartments soon. Finally buying something. Gina was hoping you could help us. You have such great taste. Frankly, I think she just wants you there to gang up on me. If we don't see eye to eye, I suspect she wants you to be the tiebreaker. Honestly, it's fine with me. Whatever she wants."

Tess put her container down. It was empty. She lay down, facing Bobby.

"It was great to see you, Tess. Thanks for listening. I'm gonna clean this stuff up. I'll leave the crackers here in case you want more," Bobby said, picking up the containers and spoons.

He walked into the kitchen and quietly said, "Man, I'm so sorry, Jack. It was hard to imagine what shape she was in until I saw her with my own eyes."

"That was the best thing that's happened here in thirty hours. Thank you," Jack replied, his voice cracking. He cleared his throat and continued, "She won't even look at me."

"Jack, I told you why," Omar said. "It's because she loves you more than anyone and she's just not ready yet."

Bobby nodded. "Every time I said your name, her eyes changed. I'm no expert, but after what I just saw, I agree with Omar."

"I hope so," Jack said.

"I was right about Bobby, and I'm right about this," Omar insisted. "Please, I know how difficult it is, but you have to trust me."

Jack nodded.

"She's so sweet, it guts me to think of someone hurting her. I can't imagine how you feel," Bobby said.

"When I find out who did this to her, I'm going to kill him," Jack said.

✦ ✦ ✦

Tess lay on the couch all night, and Jack sat in a chair watching her. Omar stumbled into the kitchen in the morning and waved Jack over.

"Why don't you go take a shower? I'll sit with her. Then you can help her like you did yesterday. I'll make her some breakfast and try to encourage her to talk."

Jack nodded.

When he returned after his shower, Omar said, "Tess, can you please get up? It's time to brush your teeth and take a shower."

She got up and walked to their bathroom, Jack following behind. "I put a fresh towel and some new clothes over there for you," he said, pointing while avoiding eye contact. "There's a scrunchie on top if you don't want to get your hair wet." He turned the shower on. "I'll be right outside the door, sweetheart. You can let me know when you're done."

He walked away and stood outside the bathroom door, which he left slightly ajar.

When Tess finished, she opened the door and stood behind him. He was about to move out of her way, but she reached out and touched his hand. He inhaled deeply, and in a gentle voice said, "I love you with my whole heart, forever. I'm here when you're ready."

She stood for a moment before moving her hand. He stepped aside and she walked past him. In the kitchen, Omar pulled out a barstool for her. "I made you some oatmeal, and there's a glass of orange juice. Please sit and try to eat a little something."

Jack caught Omar's eye and muttered, "Something happened." Before he could continue, he noticed Tess putting her hand on her neck. "Her locket, she's looking for it," he said as he darted off.

He returned a moment later and handed the necklace to Omar. "Tess, is this what you're looking for?" Omar asked, placing it in front of her. "It was a gift from Jack. It's very special to you."

She picked it up, clutched it tightly, and squeezed her eyelids shut. She opened her eyes and in a quiet voice, she said, "Jack's heart. His whole heart. Forever." She looked up. "Omar, where's Jack?"

"I'm right here, baby," Jack said, diving in front of her. "I'm right here."

She burst into tears. "Jack, I need you."

He threw his arms around her and pressed her tightly against him. "I'm right here. It's okay. I'm here. I've got you."

She couldn't stop wailing. Jack scooped her up in his arms and carried her to the couch. She didn't let go of him. He pressed his forehead to hers, stroked her hair, and quietly said, "It's okay, I'm here. I'm here."

"I'm not safe," she cried.

"Why aren't you safe?" he asked, holding her firmly.

She pulled back to look at him. He rubbed her shoulder with one hand and her face with the other. "Because he found me," she sobbed.

"Who found you?"

"I can't tell you."

"Why can't you tell me?"

Her cries were only getting louder; her whole body was shaking. Through her gasps, she said, "Because I'm afraid he'll take me away. I want to stay here with you. I just want to be with you. Please don't let anyone separate us. I'm not Essie. I'm not Essie. I'm Tess Miller. Please, Jack."

"No one is taking you anywhere. No one is going to separate us. I won't allow it, I promise. You can tell me. Who found you?"

"My father. My father found me," she said, before collapsing onto his chest.

"It's okay, baby. Everything is going to be okay. You're safe. I won't let anyone hurt you ever again. I've got you."

Ten minutes later, still curled tightly into a ball on Jack's lap, Tess muttered, "I'm so tired."

"I know, sweetheart. Let's go lie down."

"Okay," she said.

"I'm just going to talk to Omar for a minute."

"Please come right back."

Omar entered the living room and placed the orange juice and oatmeal in front of her. "Butterfly, it would be good if you took a few bites."

"I'm not hungry," she whimpered.

"Maybe you can try. At least have a little of your juice," Omar suggested.

Jack stood slowly, still holding her hand. Tess looked up at him with fearful eyes. "I promise, I'll be right back," he assured her.

Jack and Omar walked into the kitchen but remained where Tess could see them. In a hushed voice, Jack asked, "What do you know about her father?"

Omar shook his head. "Nothing. She told me her grandfather and uncle abused her. She never said a word about anyone else, only that she wanted nothing to do with anyone from her family."

"We need to find out exactly where he is. Call Bobby and ask him to locate him and to call when he has information. I'm not going to leave Tess, so tell him to call you or leave me a voicemail."

"Okay," Omar replied. "Jack, we need to know what he did to her and why she's so afraid. It's the only way to help her. After she gets some rest, I think we should try to get a proper meal into her, watch one of her favorite movies or something to relax, and if she seems like she can handle it, we need to ask her. Since you're the one she's opening up to, I think you should do it. I'll stay in your sight line and let you know if I think you should stop. She's in a fragile state, and we don't want to cause any more trauma."

"All right," Jack said.

"She might reveal that he also raped her, so we need to be prepared to hear whatever she tells us."

"Yeah, I know."

Omar put his hand on Jack's shoulder. "Now I understand why she told Vivian her name is Mrs. Miller. It's her identity. She doesn't fear what someone will do to her, but that she will be separated from you. It's important you assure her that's never going to happen. She needs to feel safe and connected. Whatever you can do to make her feel that way, you should do."

"I understand."

"And she shouldn't be alone. We don't have a complete picture of her state of mind yet. We should err on the side of caution."

"Okay, I understand."

"You haven't said much. Are you okay, Jack?"

"I am, now that Tess has come back to us. I'm just eager to be with her, to help her, to stop feeling so damn useless."

They walked back into the living room. "I drank some juice," Tess said.

Jack smiled. "Let's go get some rest, sweetheart." He took her hand and led her into their bedroom.

"I need to go to the bathroom," she said.

"I'll wait right here," he said, standing near the door.

When she came out, he took her hand and they walked over to their bed. She climbed in and lay on her side, facing him. He crawled in beside her and put his hand on her shoulder.

"How are you doing?" he asked.

"I don't know." She started to tear up.

"It's okay," he said, tucking her hair behind her ear.

"It's so lonely without you. I missed you."

"I missed you too. More than you could know." He leaned forward and lightly pressed his lips to hers.

"I missed that," she whispered.

"Me too." He kissed her again. "I love you more than anything."

"I love you too," she said. "Jack, I'm so tired."

"I know. Let's get some sleep."

"Promise you won't leave."

"I promise. I'm not going anywhere."

She turned around, and he wrapped his arms around her. They closed their eyes and were soon fast asleep.

Chapter 12

Five hours later, they awoke in exactly the same position in which they fell asleep. Tess ran her fingers against Jack's hand.

"Hey," he whispered.

"I'm going to freshen up," she said. She got up and went to the bathroom. A few minutes later, she emerged with a clean face and glistening teeth.

"My turn," Jack said, grazing her arm as he walked past her.

When he returned, Tess was curled up in the chair in the corner of the room, crying.

He rushed over, knelt before her, and took her hand. "It's okay. I'm here."

"Jack, I'm so sorry."

"You have nothing to be sorry for."

"I'm not strong like you," she sniveled.

"Tess, you're the strongest person I know. For most of my life, I had to block out all my feelings, stop seeing people. You've experienced the worst of what people can do, and you still look everyone in the eye and see their humanity.

You choose love, always. I couldn't do that. I'm in awe of you, Tess Miller. I will never be as strong as you are."

She ran her fingers through his hair.

"Gracie punctured my heart, and then you cracked it wide open. Before the two of you, I had stopped myself from feeling."

"But I'm such a terrible burden."

"That isn't true. Please don't think that for a minute."

"I can see it on your face. You're so worried and it's my fault."

"Sweetheart, of course I'm worried. I hate to see you hurting. But that doesn't mean you're a burden. I'm honored to take care of you. People who love each other take care of each other; you take care of me all the time. You're the kindest, most wonderful person I've ever known."

She shook her head. "That isn't true. I'm selfish."

"Why are you saying that?" he asked.

"Because you want to save the world, and I just want you to save me."

"Oh, sweetheart, come here." He pulled her close, and she put her arms around him. "We'll get through this. I promise. Besides, this is what I signed up to do. I will protect you from the darkness, with my whole heart, forever. For now, I think we should go eat something. You'll feel better with some food in you. Come on," he coaxed, helping her rise.

She grabbed a tissue from the nightstand to clean herself up, took his hand, and followed him into the kitchen.

"Well good afternoon, sleepyheads," Omar said. "Are you feeling more rested?"

"Uh-huh," Tess muttered.

"Something smells good in here," Jack remarked.

"I had Thai food delivered, all of Tess's favorites. Dishes and chopsticks are already set out in the living room. Jack, can you help me with the food and drinks?"

"Why don't you go sit down," Jack said to Tess. "We'll be right there."

Tess shuffled into the living room and collapsed onto the sofa.

"How's she doing?" Omar asked quietly.

"She slept, but then when I came out of the bathroom, she was crying. She told me she's not strong and she feels like a burden. It wasn't good. I don't know if I said the right things or got through to her."

"Tess has always cared more about other people than herself, so I was concerned that's where her mind would go. We'll just have to keep reinforcing the message that we love her and we're always glad to be there for her. The very last thing we want her to think is that she's a burden. That's a rabbit hole of despair."

"Any word from Bobby?" Jack asked.

"He located her father. He lives in a retirement home in Rhode Island and was admitted to a local hospital three days ago. Bobby's having trouble getting more information. He hasn't been able to confirm if he's still there. He said he'd find out and get back to us as soon as possible."

"Okay."

"The best thing we can do right now is try to get some food in her and ease her into a better frame of mind. If you'll grab the drinks, I'll bring the food in."

Jack nodded.

Omar set the containers on the coffee table. "We've got loads of pad Thai with tofu, steamed veggies, summer rolls, and peanut sauce. All your favorites, Tess. And here's chicken and rice for Jack."

"Thank you," Jack said, placing sparkling waters in front of each of them and taking a seat on the couch beside Tess.

"I figured you both must be starving," Omar said.

"Yeah," Jack agreed.

"All of a sudden, I feel famished. Everything smells good," Tess said. "Thank you."

"My pleasure," Omar replied. "Well, I thought we could use some fun, so we're going to watch one of your favorite movies. *Betty Blue* has subtitles, so that's out. You only watch *Breakfast at Tiffany's* when you're in New York, so that won't work. That leaves us with my personal favorite, our old standby, *Moulin Rouge*, which is all set and ready to go."

"Oh, I don't think Jack will like that."

"Nonsense," Omar responded.

Tess turned to Jack. "It's a love story and a musical."

"And it's Tess's favorite film," Omar added.

"If you love it, I'm sure I will too," Jack said.

Tess shrugged. "Okay."

"You have to tell me once and for all what you love most about this movie. Is it the spectacular sets?" Omar asked.

"They are wonderful, but no."

"The big musical numbers?"

"Also wonderful, but no."

"Then it must be the message, that to love and be loved is the greatest gift of all."

"I do love that, but no. I'm not telling."

"Butterfly, did you ever tell Jack about that time in Chicago?" Omar asked, plopping down in a recliner.

After a pause, Tess began, "I had been on the road for what seemed like ages doing book events. Omar was busy with grad school, so I hadn't seen him in months, which was torture, so we were going to meet in Chicago. Somewhere in Illinois, I got a nasty cold. By the time I got to Chicago, I was deathly sick."

"And let me tell you, Jack, she's an absolute monster when she doesn't feel well."

"I can't believe that," Jack said.

"Oh, it's true. First, there's the nightmare of getting her to admit that she's ill. Then there's taking care of her. She gets very grumpy. It's brutal."

Tess giggled. "It's true. I hate being sick."

"The only good thing that happens when you get sick is that it reminds me you're human. You're so impossibly wonderful all the time, that sometimes I wonder. Then you get a cold and turn into a little beast. It's quite reassuring."

Tess smiled. "Being the marvelous friend that he is, Omar stayed with me in my hotel suite since I wasn't up to going out. We ordered loads of room service, all junk, including baskets of french fries, and we watched *Moulin Rouge* for like the fifth time."

"Nice try, it was more like the twenty-fifth time," Omar countered.

"Wait, you ate french fries?" Jack asked Tess.

She nodded. "A whole basket of them. I was so loopy from the cold medicine I didn't know what I was doing, or maybe I didn't care. Omar wanted to cheer me up, so he acted out every single musical number in the entire movie. I mean, dancing and belting out every song. I had been so grouchy, yet I couldn't help but laugh and smile. It was splendid. Thank goodness he has a gorgeous voice."

"And then of course there's 'Your Song,' which you and I always do together. I sing, we both dance. Even sick as a dog, I made you get out of bed for that one."

Tess laughed. "I remember." She paused and looked a bit melancholy. "We had some fun times."

"And we'll have many more, Butterfly."

"I hope so," she replied.

"I think it's time to hit play," Omar said, grabbing the remote. "Take some food, guys."

Tess helped herself to a modest portion of pad Thai and steamed vegetables. She ate slowly while the movie played.

When her dish was empty, she took more pad Thai and a summer roll. Omar smiled inconspicuously at Jack.

Right before "Your Song" came on, Omar said, "You know what's coming."

"Oh, I don't think I'm up to it," Tess said.

"Well I am. You're not going to leave me on my own, are you?"

The song began and Omar leapt up, took Tess's hand, and began singing to her. When he belted out the words "if they're green or they're blue," she stood up, smiling. They started dancing across the room, in perfect unison with the film. At one point, Omar jumped onto a chair and opened an umbrella he had stashed away. Tess laughed. Jack watched, grinning from ear to ear, relief and love washing over him. At the end, Omar twirled Tess out and back to him, spun her up in his arms, and then came the grand dip. When she stood upright, they were both smiling and laughing. Jack clapped.

"We've never done that for an audience before," Tess said. She sat down and looked at Omar. "What would I do without you?"

"You'll never have to find out," he replied.

Tess nestled into Jack, and they watched the rest of the movie. When it was over, she looked up at him expectantly. "Well, what did you think?"

"It was great. But I have to say, my favorite part was your dance with Omar. You two have such a beautiful friendship."

"Yeah, I got pretty lucky with men later in life," she said.

"How about some tea, guys?" Omar asked.

"Sure," Tess replied.

"I'll put the leftovers away and make a pot," he said.

"I'll help you," Jack offered.

"I've got it. You stay with Tess," Omar said.

Tess and Jack cuddled on the couch. He stroked her hair and asked, "How are you doing?"

"Better."

He placed a delicate kiss on the top of her head.

Soon, Omar returned with a tray carrying a teapot and cups. "It's chamomile. That's soothing," he said, pouring it into the teacups.

Tess sat up. "Thank you."

Omar took his seat and nodded at Jack.

"Sweetheart, we wanted to talk to you."

"What's wrong?" she asked, turning to him.

"Nothing's wrong. We don't want to upset you, so if you're not up to it, it's perfectly okay," he said, rubbing her back. "We just wanted to ask you a couple of questions. About your father, Tess. It would help me protect you if I knew a little more."

"Okay," she said softly.

"What did he say when he called?"

"He just said, 'Hello, Essie.' I told him, 'I don't want to talk to you.' Then he said, 'If you don't talk to me, I'm going to call your husband.' I got scared and hung up. Then I smashed my phone so he couldn't call back. I'm sorry, I guess my phone is ruined."

"That's okay. We can get you a new one," Jack said. He glanced up at Omar, who gestured for him to continue. He took Tess's hands, caressing her fingers. "I would never ask you anything to hurt you; I only want to help you. You know that, right?"

"Yes."

"Sweetheart, when you were growing up, did your father hurt you like your uncle and grandfather did?"

"No. Never."

Relief started to sweep across Jack's face, but then Tess continued, "What he did was much worse. It's the worst thing anyone has ever done to me."

Jack held Tess's face in both of his hands. He swallowed and said, "You can tell me."

"I couldn't take it anymore. So, I summoned all the strength I had, and I went to my father to tell him what was happening. I told him what they did to me. Jack, I told him everything I could manage to say out loud." Her eyes began to tear, but she continued, speaking very slowly as if she was reliving it. "I told him how they would bring me to the basement, lock the door, make me take off my clothes, and cover my head, and then I told him the terrible things they did to me. I told him how I begged them to stop." Jack saw Omar stand up, sobbing so hard he had to turn away. Jack's eyes flooded, but he held her face, looking straight into her eyes. "I told him, and he said, 'Okay.' I thought that meant it was over, that he would do something. But he didn't do anything. He let them do whatever they wanted. They were welcome in that house any time. Maybe he didn't believe me or maybe he just didn't care. What he did to me was that he did *nothing*. *Nothing* to save me from the darkness."

Jack pulled her to his chest, his arms huddled around her head. "I'm so sorry. I'm so sorry," he said through his tears.

"Nothing changed after that day, except they didn't lock the door anymore," she whimpered.

"I'm so sorry, Tess. You're safe now. I promise."

"Did I help?" she asked.

"Yeah, baby. You helped."

He held Tess for a long time, until her breathing had slowed to normal and her body relaxed. After comforting Tess, Jack leaned back, looked into her eyes, and gently asked, "Are you okay?"

"Yeah."

"Why don't you drink your tea and try to relax. Do you want me to put the TV on?"

"Okay," she replied.

He put it on and handed her the remote. "Find something light to watch. I'll be right back."

She took the remote and started flipping through stations. Jack walked into the kitchen and found Omar on the floor in the far corner of the room. He was having trouble catching his breath. Jack rushed over, knelt down, and put his hands on Omar's shoulders. "Try to slow your breath. Try to slow your breath. Deep breaths in . . . and out. Focus on your breathing. That's it," he said, and Omar's breathing steadied.

"They covered her head, Jack. They covered her head." Omar gasped.

"I know."

"How could anyone do that to her?"

Jack shook his head.

Omar said, "That's why she can't walk past a stranger without looking them in the eyes. Outside of Shelby's that night when that homeless man said, 'Someone must have taught you to do unto others,' she replied, 'Someone taught me there are no others.' *This* is what she meant. *This* is how they taught her. *This* is why she sees the humanity in each person. Because it was denied to her with such brutality."

Jack sighed. "Yeah."

"I'm sorry," Omar said, sniffling and wiping his eyes. "It's just so painful to imagine anyone hurting her like that. The damage they've done."

"I know."

"I'm all right now," Omar said, rising. "We should sit with Tess."

"Why don't you go splash some water on your face? Take a minute for yourself. I'm going to call Bobby, but I'll stay nearby."

Omar nodded and walked off.

Jack dialed Bobby's number. When Bobby answered, Jack quietly said, "Did you find her father? I just found out what he did to her."

"He's dead, Jack. He died early this morning. Cancer. That's why I had trouble getting info from the hospital— they were waiting to inform his next of kin."

"Okay, thanks," Jack said. "I'll talk to you tomorrow."

Jack waited for Omar to return. "Her father's dead. It happened early this morning."

"He must have wanted to speak to her before he died," Omar surmised.

"Yeah," Jack agreed. "Maybe Tess will feel better if we tell her. She won't have to be afraid anymore."

"We do need to tell her, but there's no way to know how she will feel. It's always complex with family, which is why this kind of abuse is so horrific. I don't know what her response will be."

They joined Tess in the living room. Jack sat beside her on the couch. She put her tea down and looked at him. He smiled dimly. "What is it?" she asked.

Omar grabbed the remote control and turned off the TV.

"Sweetheart, your father died," Jack said.

A look of confusion swept across her face. "Jack, you didn't do something . . ."

"No, baby. He died early this morning. He had cancer."

She sat silently for a moment before saying, "So, he knew he was dying when he called?"

"Yes," Jack replied.

"Do you think he was calling to apologize?" she asked.

"I don't know."

"I'm glad I hung up. Now I can always imagine he was calling to say he was sorry."

Chapter 13

The next morning, Jack and Tess lay in bed, snuggling. "How are you feeling, sweetheart?" Jack asked.

"Like I just want to stay like this for as long as possible, with you."

"There's nowhere else we need to be," he replied.

"Since we found each other, this is my favorite thing: just lying in your arms quietly, feeling so close."

"For me too."

An hour later, they rolled out of bed. Omar was in the kitchen reading the newspaper, containers of berries and a basket of fruit on the bar. He put the paper down. "Well, good morning. Butterfly, you've given me a complex about my cooking, so I went out and bought you some fruit for breakfast."

She kissed the top of his head. "Thank you."

"I'll make a fresh pot of coffee," Jack said.

"Then after breakfast, perhaps we can go out and get some fresh air. It would be good for you, Tess," Omar said.

"Okay," she agreed.

Omar smiled. "I was hoping you would say that. I took the liberty of calling Denise and making you an appointment for your blowout, since you missed your usual time. She found a way to squeeze you into her jammed schedule. Perk of being a celeb and her favorite client."

"Is that your way of saying I'm having a bad hair day?" she asked.

"Well, I don't want to kick you while you're down, but it's dreadful. I mean really, Butterfly, we have standards to adhere to."

Tess giggled, picked a grape out of the basket, and flung it at his head.

Jack grinned, taking in the lighthearted scene.

"I thought I could keep you company at the salon and Jack could go down the block to get you a new cell phone."

"How does that sound, sweetheart?" Jack asked.

"Fine," Tess said, biting into a strawberry.

Later, Jack and Omar escorted Tess to the hair salon. They barely had time to sit down in the waiting area when Denise came bounding out to greet Tess. She pulled her away so quickly that Jack and Omar couldn't say a word.

Omar turned to Jack. "You should go get her phone so you'll be back here when she's done. I called ahead, and it should be ready to pick up."

Jack's face looked pained.

"She'll be fine," Omar assured him. "I'm right here, and you'll only be a couple of blocks away."

Jack reluctantly nodded and left. Forty-five minutes later, he returned with a phone and a whole bag of accessories. "How's she doing?" he asked, taking the seat beside Omar.

"She's been blabbing on and on with Denise like they always do. This was the perfect way to start to reintegrate her into normal life. She'll be done any minute."

Tess appeared from the back of the salon. "So, what do you think? Am I suitable for viewing?"

"Gorgeous, Butterfly," Omar said. "Much better than that bird's nest you were sporting."

She laughed and playfully hit his arm. "You're terrible." She turned to Jack. "And what do you think, Mr. Miller?"

"I think you're perfect, Mrs. Miller."

When they got back to the house, Omar said, "What do you feel like doing, Butterfly? You haven't written in days. Maybe you want to try. Or if you're not up to it, we could torture Jack with some more of our favorite movies."

"You are the absolute sweetest and I couldn't survive without you, but I think you should go home," she replied.

"I'm happy to stay here as long as you like," he assured her.

"I know, and I love you for it, but you have a handsome man of your own waiting at home. He probably thinks you defected by now!" she joked.

Jack and Omar looked at her with serious expressions.

"It's okay. I'm with Jack. I feel lighter than I have in days—in years, really," she said.

"You know I'm just a phone call away," Omar said, taking her hand. "I can be here in a heartbeat."

She hugged him. "I know. I love you more than words."

"Sweetheart, do you mind if I speak with Omar for a minute?" Jack asked.

She smiled. "Of course not. I'm going to go get comfy and change into sweats."

Tess left the room, and Jack turned to Omar. "I'm just worried about her. She seems a lot better today, but . . ."

"I know," Omar replied. "It's going to take time. She's been through an intense trauma, and she's still processing it.

Just be with her. She feels safe with you. It would be good for Tess to start working again too. Writing has always been her truest friend. I don't think she should be alone for at least a few more days, maybe longer."

"We can hang out here for the rest of the weekend, and then I'll just call out of work again next week," Jack said.

"That's one option, but I'm not sure it's the best plan. She needs normalcy, and part of that is you returning to work. Is it possible for her to go to work with you? Do you have a desk or office or somewhere she could write? That way she'd have to get up in the morning and start working, and she'd have some independence, but you could keep an eye on her."

"Yes, there's a conference room two doors down from my office. She could come all week, or longer. She can see Joe and Bobby too. I can keep everyone else out of there."

"That sounds perfect. Bring it up when the time is right and see what she thinks," Omar suggested.

Jack nodded. "Omar, I don't know how to thank you for everything. We could never have gotten through this without you."

"There's no need. Tess is my family, and now you are too. I would do anything for her, and you as well. Please, don't hesitate for a minute to call. I can be back here any time."

"Thank you," Jack said.

Jack and Tess spent the rest of the afternoon watching TV and eating leftover Thai food. The next morning, they exercised together before breakfast. Tess took a mug of coffee and said she was going up to her office. Jack followed behind with the Sunday newspaper. When he walked into the office, Tess was standing at her desk, hesitantly brushing her fingertips across the top of her laptop. He kissed her on the cheek. "Why don't you try writing?"

"Oh, I don't know," she mumbled.

"Well, you can try if you want to. I have this to get through," he said, holding up the large newspaper. "I'll be over there in the corner. If you get bored, you can come hang out with me."

He ambled to the far side of the room, sat down, and opened the newspaper. Tess sat at her desk, staring at him. Finally, she put on her reading glasses, opened her laptop, and began working. Two hours later, she turned off her computer, strolled over to Jack, and plopped onto his lap.

"How's it going, baby?" he asked.

"It's going. But I'm done for today. Let's go watch a movie or something. I'll miss you so much tomorrow when you go back to work."

"Actually, I was hoping you'd come with me. There's an empty office you can use, and that way we can see each other all day."

She smiled. "I like the sound of that."

"Good," he said, kissing her.

Chapter 14

On Monday morning, they were both in their bathroom getting ready to go to Jack's office for the day. Tess was standing in front of the vanity, putting on her makeup, when Jack came up behind her and dropped a kiss in her hair.

"I'm almost ready," she said.

"Take your time. I'll go make coffee."

Jack slipped out of the room. He turned the coffee pot on, pulled his phone out of his pocket, and called Joe.

"Good morning," Joe answered.

"Hi, Joe. I just wanted to make sure everything is all set for Tess."

"I came in early and told everyone the conference room is off-limits for the week."

"Thank you."

"Glad to help. How's Tess doing?" Joe asked.

"Okay, I think." He sighed. "I hope so at least."

"I'm looking forward to seeing her. Bobby was planning to get takeout so the four of us could have lunch together, if you think that's a good idea."

"Yeah, that would be great. Thank you. We'll see you soon."

"See you soon."

Just as Jack hung up, the coffee machine beeped and Tess strolled into the room wearing jeans, a white button-down shirt, and black blazer.

"You look nice," Jack remarked.

"Thank you, baby," she replied, giving him a quick kiss.

"The coffee is ready. Do you want me to make oatmeal?"

She shook her head. "Let's just take the coffee in tumblers and go."

"Sweetheart, we have some time if you want to have breakfast."

"I'm not hungry, but if you are . . ."

"I can grab something at the office, it's just . . ." He paused and rubbed her shoulders. "I'm concerned you're not eating enough."

"Jack, I'm fine. I'm not hungry. Please, let's just go," she replied, grabbing her workbag.

Jack and Tess walked into the office and were immediately greeted by Joe.

"Great to see you, Tess," he said, giving her a peck on the cheek.

"You too," she replied.

"You class the place up," he remarked.

She giggled.

"I'm going to get Tess situated," Jack said.

Jack led Tess into the oval-shaped conference room, with glass windows all around overlooking cubicles and other offices. He set up her laptop at the table. "There's coffee and tea over there," he said, pointing to the kitchenette. "You know where my office is, just around the corner."

"Thanks. I'll be fine," she said.

"I'll stop in to check on you, but you can come get me anytime you need me."

"Okay."

"Bobby, Joe, and I will have lunch with you later. Bobby's going to pick something up. What do you want?"

"Oh, uh, just some fruit would be fine. Thank you."

There was a knock on the door, and Bobby came vaulting in. "Hey, you," he said to Tess with a huge hug. "So glad you're feeling better."

"Thank you for everything."

"Nah, that's what friends are for. Well, I don't want to intrude. I just wanted to say hi and welcome. I'll stop in again later, and you can always find me if you want to," he said, leaving the room.

"Hey, come here," Jack said when they were alone, pulling her near. He embraced her tightly. "I guess I should get to work if you don't need anything."

"I'm fine, really," she insisted.

He left the room but stopped outside the door to peer in. Tess had already put on her reading glasses and begun typing. He took a deep breath and went to his office. Joe was waiting for him.

"Tess looks good," Joe said. "You're a different story. You look like you've been through the ringer."

"I'm just worried about her. I don't like leaving her alone."

"It's good for her to work. She knows how to find you. Try not to worry. Bobby and I will check in on her too. She's safe here."

"Thanks," Jack mumbled.

Between Jack, Joe, and Bobby, someone stopped in to check on Tess every half hour. At noon, they came bounding into the room with lunch. Bobby placed two white paper bags on the table.

"I must have lost track of time," Tess said, taking off her glasses and closing her laptop.

Joe smiled discreetly at Jack.

"Hi, sweetheart," Jack said, kissing the top of her head and taking the seat beside her. "How's your day going?"

"It's going. What about you?"

"Pretty uneventful around here, which is always a good thing," he replied.

Bobby started doling out the food. He placed a colorful fruit salad in front of Tess and slid sandwiches to Jack and Joe. Then he took out two extra sandwiches. He unwrapped one of them. "Jack said you eat grilled cheese with pickles in it, which is super weird. I like weird, so I decided to try it. It's my second sandwich, so I'm only going to eat half of it. You're welcome to have the other half," he said, placing it between them.

"Thanks," she said, picking up her half and biting into it.

Bobby took a mouthful. "Wow, this is actually really good. I'd never have thought of it. So, what are you working on, Tess?"

"Years ago, I wrote a collection of essays about the power of literature. My publisher has been trying to get me to release a new edition for ages, and I finally agreed. It's perfect timing, actually. I could use a little break from fiction, which is so much more draining."

They spent the next half hour talking and eating. Joe and Bobby picked up the garbage while Jack had a moment with Tess.

"You doing okay?" he asked, stroking her arm.

"Yeah. Baby, you don't have to worry so much. I promise."

"You know where to find me if you need me. I love you."

"I love you too."

Tess opened her laptop and put her glasses back on. The guys left the room. As soon as the door was shut, Jack said, "Holy shit, Bobby, you're like the food whisperer."

Bobby laughed. "Glad to help."

"She really seems like she's doing as well as she could be, under the circumstances," Joe remarked.

"Yeah," Jack agreed, visibly more relaxed.

Tess continued working for the next two and a half hours, and Jack, Bobby, and Joe continued to pop in to say hello. Just after three o'clock, Chris walked into the conference room, ostensibly to get a cup of coffee.

"Hi, Tess," he said.

"Hello," she replied, busy on her keyboard.

"I guess I didn't get the memo that it's bring-your-wife-to-work day. I suppose when you're the boss, you think you can do whatever you want, huh?"

"What?" Tess asked.

"Oh, nothing. I mean, Jack's the man. If he wants you here, that's his call. I just don't think it looks very good for him. See ya!"

He took his coffee and left.

Tess noticed Bobby walking by, and she jumped up and swung the door open.

"Hey, Tess. Are you okay?" Bobby asked.

"Is it bad for Jack that I'm here? Please, you have to tell me the truth."

"No, not at all. What are you talking about?"

"Chris just came into the conference room and told me that it wasn't good for Jack that I'm here. The last thing I want is to cause trouble for him or to be a burden. Should I leave?"

"Absolutely not. Please, just sit tight. I'll be right back."

Bobby made a beeline to Jack's office, where Jack and Joe were reviewing a document. "Jack, please stay calm, but something happened."

Jack jumped up, panic in his eyes.

"Apparently, Chris went into the conference room and said something to Tess about how her being here is causing a problem for you."

"He did *what*?" Jack bellowed.

"She asked me if it was a burden for you that she's here."

A look of rage washed across his face. He opened his top desk drawer, pulled out a gun, and sprinted out of the room before anyone could stop him.

Bobby and Joe followed, hollering, "Jack, you need to calm down!"

Tess watched as he flew by the conference room.

Jack dragged Chris out of his chair and slammed him against the wall, jamming an arm under his neck. "What the fuck did you say to my wife?" he screamed.

Chris was too stunned to reply.

"Jack, calm down. Think about what you're doing," Joe pleaded.

"What the fuck did you say to her?" Jack screeched.

Tess heard the commotion and came running over just as Jack jammed his gun into Chris's temple and screamed, "I'll fucking kill you. Nobody hurts her!"

Tess was trembling. "Jack, please, put the gun down. I'm not hurt."

"You're scaring Tess," Bobby said. "Put the gun down."

Tess walked up to Jack, placed her hand on his shoulder, and softly said, "Please, Jack. Put the gun down. Please, baby."

Jack was still shaking, but he lowered the gun. He

stepped back, let Chris go, and handed the weapon to Bobby. He turned to Tess but couldn't look her in the eyes. "I'm sorry. I'm sorry."

"It's okay," she said. "Let's walk away."

"We should go back to the conference room," he mumbled. Tess wrapped an arm around him and led him back to the conference room. "I'm sorry," he said again. "Please stay here. I just need a minute."

He went to his office where Bobby was waiting for him. He shut the door, hunched over, and broke down into tears. "I can't believe I did that. What's wrong with me? She already thinks it's bad for me to have her here, and now I've proved it to her because I can't fucking control myself." He covered his face with his hands. "I've made everything worse."

"Jack, try to take a beat. You were just trying to protect her," Bobby said.

"This is my fault. It's all my fault. Tess is scared and traumatized because of me."

Joe let himself in and closed the door behind him. "Listen, I told Chris what's going on."

"You know how private she is. Why did you do that?" Jack asked, still hysterical.

"I didn't tell him the details, just that Tess was the victim of a crime and that she's here so you can keep an eye on her. He felt terrible. He's not going to file a report. No one who saw what happened is going to say anything."

Jack tried to regain his composure, but his face was bright red and his breathing was out of control. "I don't know what to say to Tess to fix this."

"Let me talk to her," Joe offered.

"I don't know," Jack replied, pacing.

"Listen, I didn't tell either of you this, but I had a health scare a few months ago. They thought it might be cancer.

I needed to bring someone with me to the oncologist, so I asked Tess."

"She never told me that," Jack said.

"I asked her to keep it private. It turned out to be a false alarm, but we spent hours waiting and talking. She told me how traumatic her childhood was and that being with you is the first time she's felt truly safe or happy. I confessed to her that I am lonely and that watching you two together makes me wish I had someone to share my life with. I asked her what it is that makes your bond so strong, and without missing a beat, she said, 'Like a puzzle, our broken pieces fit together.'"

Joe's words seemed to comfort Jack, who was slowly pulling himself together.

"She knows you're not perfect, Jack. Please, let me go talk to her. I think I can help."

Jack nodded.

Joe knocked on the door to the conference room before opening it. Tess was walking in circles. "Is Jack okay?" she asked with wide eyes.

"He feels very bad for upsetting you and he's ashamed of himself, but he'll be okay. May I speak with you for a minute?"

"Of course."

"Please, let's sit down," he suggested, pulling out her chair. "Jack is feeling especially protective of you right now because you've gone through something so painful. It's natural that he would feel that way. He loves you, Tess. Chris is a massive jerk; you know he's been riding Jack for a long time. It has nothing to do with you. Emotions are high, so things got a little out of hand, but the last thing Jack wants is for you to think that you're causing a problem for him. Nothing could be further from the truth. The best thing you can do for him is to try to move past what happened here. Will you please stay?"

"Okay," she said.

Joe smiled. "Thank you, Tess. I'll let you get back to your work."

She grabbed his arm. "Please keep an eye on him for me."

"I will."

Joe smiled and left the room. After he shut the door, he saw Tess put on her glasses and open her laptop. He went back to Jack's office.

"She's fine," he said.

"Are you sure?" Jack asked.

"Yes. She's working. You can go see for yourself. She asked me to keep an eye on *you*. She's worried about you."

"Thank you," Jack said, and he went to go check on Tess. He stood in the hall and watched her typing. He took a deep breath and slunk away before she could see him.

For the rest of the day, Tess kept working and Bobby and Joe stopped by occasionally to check on her, but Jack stayed holed up in his office and kept his distance. Tired of waiting for him, Tess got up to stretch her legs and found herself in Jack's office. "Hey, stranger. How are you holding up?"

"Hey," he said, coming around his desk to greet her. "I'm so sorry, sweetheart."

"You don't have to be sorry," she said, reaching out for his hand. "I just want to know you're all right."

"I feel awful for upsetting you. I completely lost it."

"Chris is an ass," Tess said.

He laughed.

"But Jack, that's not really what's going on here. This wasn't about Chris."

He looked down, unable to meet her gaze.

"I'm so sorry I didn't realize how traumatic this has been for you, the toll it's taken, and—"

"No, sweetheart," he interrupted, "this isn't about me. I just want to take care of you. Please don't worry about me."

"Jack, I know your instinct is to always put me first, but this is about you. You've gone through something terrible too. Pretending nothing happened won't help either of us. I think we need to talk about everything that's happened." He took a breath and she continued. "Please, honey. For me."

He brushed his fingers across her cheek. "Okay."

"Let's go home."

✦ ✦ ✦

They walked into their house and Tess dropped her bag on the counter and held Jack's hand, leading him to the living room. She took her shoes off and he followed suit. "Get cozy with me," she said.

He lay down on the couch, his head propped up on throw pillows, and opened his arms. She curled up against him, draping her arm across his body.

"This feels so good," she said.

"It sure does," he agreed, dropping a kiss in her hair.

"Baby, we need to talk about what happened."

"When I heard what Chris said to you, I completely lost my shit."

"Yes, you did." She looked straight into his eyes. "But we both know it wasn't about Chris. You want to save me from things that happened decades ago, from the people who did hurt me. But you can't."

He looked down.

"Jack, you can't. What's in the past can't be changed. Knowing vaguely about it is one thing, but hearing all the details may have been too much, and—"

"Hey," he interrupted, rubbing her arm and looking

into her eyes, "I wanted you to tell me. You can always tell me anything."

"It was still a lot to process. I want you to know that I understand why you're feeling so protective."

"It's just . . ." He stopped himself.

"What? Tell me how you're feeling."

"I don't want to make this about me and . . ." She waited patiently for him to continue. "I'm afraid of saying the wrong thing."

"Jack, we love and trust each other. There's nothing we can't share. If it's how you feel, it can't be wrong. Please say whatever's on your mind. The only way out is through."

He took a breath and looked deeply into her eyes. "I've spent my whole life protecting people from imminent danger, external threats. That's what I'm good at. Today with Chris, it felt like something I could handle. Protecting you from the past, from what's inside your own mind . . . I don't know how to do that."

She gave him a soft kiss. "Thank you, baby. I know it wasn't easy for you to share that with me. I understand more than you may realize." She gave his bicep a squeeze. "Don't you think I feel something every day when I see the scars on your body? Don't you think I would give anything to take that pain away? But I know that I can't, so instead, they remind me to show you every single day how much I love you, and to always be gentle with you. Can you please try to do the same thing? You can't save me from the past, but you can be with me now, love me now. Just love me. That's all I want."

He brushed his fingers across her cheek. "Yes, I can do that."

Chapter 15

The next morning, Tess woke up first and quietly slipped out of bed.

As she meandered to the bathroom, Jack mumbled, "You taking a shower?"

"Uh-huh. Get a little more sleep."

After Tess got ready for the day, she found Jack waiting in the bedroom. "Your turn, honey," she said.

Jack grazed her hand as he passed by. Twenty minutes later, he came into the kitchen and found Tess sticking an empty oatmeal bowl in the sink. He smiled to himself. "Here," she said, handing him a coffee tumbler and something wrapped in foil, and they headed to his office.

Jack, Joe, and Bobby checked on Tess less frequently than they had the previous day. Everyone was settling into a comfortable routine. At noon, they came into the conference room with a huge platter of sushi. Bobby distributed chopsticks, paper plates, and bottled water. Tess was leaning against the wall, talking on her cell phone.

"Hang on a minute," she said to the person on the phone. She turned to Jack. "Hi, baby."

He kissed her. "What's going on?"

"There might be a bidding war for the Chinese translation rights to my new book."

"That's great, sweetheart."

She smiled. "I just need a couple of minutes to finish this call, fellas. Please eat, I'll be right there."

"We'll wait," Bobby said as he and Joe sat down.

Tess shifted her focus back to her phone call. "Hey, Crystal. Please read his message." She listened for a moment and then said, "Wow, respect and loyalty? That almost made me laugh out loud. Let me think." She closed her eyes in thought and then said, "Okay, here's my response. Are you ready? Dear Tihao, Thank you for your interest in expanding our relationship. I'm sure you know that the only reason we are having this conversation is because I operate from a place of respect and loyalty. That does not mean, however, that I have replaced my backbone with a wishbone. The terms we offered are fair and nonnegotiable. We both know that if I allow this to go to an open bidding war, the price will be much higher. I trust we are clear on what the deal is. I don't want any last-minute changes. Beyond the royalty structure, there is a non-recoupable licensing fee. Do not attempt to roll it into an advance. If you're going to use words like respect and loyalty, you should honor them. Please stop dragging your feet. You have seventy-two hours to send a signed contract. Otherwise, we'll go to an open bid and I'll spend my next holiday in Beijing or Shanghai instead of Taipei. I look forward to hearing from you directly, not from your lawyers." Tess paused. "Crystal, did you get all that? Okay, add a paragraph at the end that reads: I hope your mother is doing well. You are all in my thoughts. Tess." She paused and said, "Yup, that's it. Please send it immediately. Gotta go. Bye."

Tess hung up, and Jack pulled out a chair for her to take a seat. Bobby and Joe stared with their mouths agape.

"Sorry about that," she said.

"That was awesome," Bobby said.

"What?" Tess asked.

"It's just that you're literally the nicest person we know, but you're such a badass. I mean, 'I haven't replaced my backbone with a wishbone' and the 'respect and loyalty' stuff. Savage. Priceless."

Tess laughed.

"I'm in awe," Joe said. "Truly, you're the most impressive person I've ever met, Tess."

She blushed. "You're overly kind."

"Not at all. I sincerely mean it. I've thought it since the day I met you."

Jack rubbed Tess's back. "I know. I'm more amazed by her every day."

"And then you asked about his mother and sounded so genuine," Bobby said. "How do you do that when someone's jerking you around?"

"His mother has Alzheimer's. It's very difficult for him. He is simultaneously someone with whom I'm having a professional wrestling match and also a human being who is dealing with a difficult personal situation. I can hold two thoughts." She cracked open her water bottle and took a sip.

"I can't stare at this sushi anymore without devouring it. Let's eat," Joe said, gesturing toward the platter. "Tess, the veggie rolls are in front of you."

"Thank you," she said as they all helped themselves.

"Why not let it go to a bidding war and drive up the price?" Bobby asked.

"I know which publisher I want to work with for reasons that are more important to me than financial terms. For example, we'll have an easier time slipping past the censors with a Taiwanese publisher. If I allow it to go to an open bid, there's tremendous pressure to take the highest offer. If I don't, it puts me in a terrible spot for future negotiations. I'm trying to make this happen beforehand, so I can control the outcome."

"Tess, I've always been curious about your approach to negotiations. I've heard that the two most important things are the ability to walk away and being armed with information. Do you agree?" Joe asked.

"That's the common wisdom, but no, I don't agree. It's better if you're able to walk away, but that isn't always the case. Sometimes we have to play ball with people whether we like it or not. I'm sure you encounter that in your work all the time. And having as much information as you can is certainly a good thing, but the facts aren't always on your side. Most people rely on those two things to win negotiations, but they will betray you because you can't control them. You should walk into every negotiation with something you can control. There's a third factor that I think is most important at the end of the day, and that's the story, the vision you are selling. The more you believe it, the better you can persuade others, even when the facts don't support you."

"Brilliant," Joe said.

"That's my Tess," Jack said, staring lovingly at her.

"It's not just business either. Do you remember the story my friend Abdul told you at our wedding about passing through that mob?"

They nodded.

"My goal in that situation was to make sure he was safe. The facts were certainly not on our side, nor were we able to walk away and avoid it. Despite the advice from the security team, it was clear to me that the situation was going to get worse and we needed to move as quickly as possible. But first, I needed to make Abdul believe we could do it. So, we chanted until I could see that he believed. That's how we made it through that day. Of course, something terrible could have happened to us anyway, but without him believing it was possible to get to the other side in one piece, we wouldn't have had a chance."

"Did you believe?" Jack asked softly.

She looked at him. "That there's only darkness and light and that love is the bridge between them? Yes, with all my heart."

Jack smiled. "Thank God you made it."

"So Tess, do you think you'll get that Chinese contract you want?" Bobby asked.

"Yes, within twenty-four hours, and I'll hear from Tihao before that, likely trying to smooth things over. It's a little after noon here, which means it's midnight in Taipei. Tihao suffers from insomnia and often scrolls through his emails when he's up at night. If that's the case, I could hear from him any minute. If not, I'll get an email first thing in the morning his time."

"Keep us posted," Bobby said.

"Please do," Joe added.

Tess smiled. "So, what are you guys doing today to keep America safe?"

Twenty minutes later as they were wrapping up lunch, Tess glanced at her phone. She giggled.

"Something good?" Jack asked.

"I'll let Bobby do the honors," she said, handing him her phone.

Bobby read the email aloud for the group. "Dear Tess, My sincere apologies for the delay in sending the contract.

Yes, the terms you outlined are acceptable. You will have the signed contract by the end of the business day. Thank you for granting us this opportunity. It is our great honor to continue bringing your work to Chinese and Taiwanese audiences. We hold you in the highest esteem and feel fortunate to work with you. My mother is doing as well as she can be. Thank you for inquiring. The lavender oil you sent helps soothe her. That was very thoughtful. I hope to see you in Taipei again soon. Warm wishes, Tihao." Bobby slid the phone back to Tess. "Damn, you called it."

Tess smiled.

"Well done, baby," Jack said, leaning over to kiss her.

"So Tess, I'll be picking up lunch tomorrow. Any special requests?" Joe asked.

"Thank you, but I won't be here."

"Sweetheart, what are you talking about?" Jack asked, visibly surprised.

She turned to face him. "I have to go to the library to do research for my book. I'm a week behind." She then turned to the group. "You've all been very sweet, and it's lovely having lunch with three handsome men, but we all have things to do."

"Well, we'll sure miss having you here," Bobby said. "Come back anytime you want."

Jack grabbed Tess's hand. "I can take the day off and go with you tomorrow."

"Nonsense. You have a job to do. With all the time you're spending with me, I'm seriously beginning to worry about the safety of this country," she said with a giggle. "I don't need a chaperone. I'll be fine."

"We can talk more about this later," he said, concern emanating from every syllable.

"We can talk later, but it won't change anything. We all need to get on with life," she replied.

"Jack, let's clean this up and let Tess get back to work," Joe suggested.

Bobby started clearing away the garbage. "Congrats again on your deal, Tess. You're a total boss."

Jack kissed Tess and followed his friends out of the room.

"Relax," Joe said, placing his hand on Jack's shoulder.

They all walked to Jack's office. As soon as he shut the door, he said with panic in his eyes, "It's too soon."

"For whom, you or Tess?" Joe asked.

Jack stared daggers at him.

"I didn't mean it that way. It's just that she seems okay. I mean, my God, did you hear her on the phone?"

"Joe's right," Bobby agreed. "She was on fire."

"That's different," Jack protested, his face creased with worry.

"You have to let her live her life. Maybe closing that deal was just what she needed to feel like her old self again," Joe said. "If you truly don't think she's ready, talk to her tonight and convince her not to go alone. But this isn't the place for it. You'll just upset her."

Jack took a deep breath. "I appreciate everything you've both said and done. You should get back to work."

As soon as they left his office, Jack called Omar.

"Hello?"

"It's Jack. Tess wants to go to the library alone tomorrow."

"I know. She texted me an hour ago."

"I'm worried about her being alone," Jack said.

"I understand, but I think you have to let her do this. We can't treat her like a child. The fact is that she hasn't tried to harm herself, and she seems to be doing remarkably well considering everything that's happened. It's good that she wants to work."

"How do you know she won't slip into a bad state of mind and that something won't happen to her?" Jack asked.

"I don't know. We can never know that with certainty. But she's a highly capable adult, and we have to trust her. We need to make sure she will tell us honestly how she's doing and will ask for help if she needs it. That's all we can do."

"I don't like it," Jack said.

"I know it's hard because it's all still fresh, but it will get easier."

"Yeah, okay. Thank you."

"Bye," Omar said.

"Bye."

After hanging up, Jack picked up the framed wedding photo on his desk, held it against his chest, and prayed that Omar was right.

✦ ✦ ✦

When they got home, they made a quick dinner together and ate in front of the TV. The moment they were done, Tess said, "Let's go to bed." She disappeared into their bathroom and reemerged wearing a white silk slip.

"Wow, what's this?" he asked.

"We haven't been together in a week. We usually can't make it through the day."

He took her hand and looked down. "I know, but . . ."

"Don't you still want to be with me?" she asked.

He put his hands on her hips. "More than anything. I just don't want to hurt you."

"You can't," she said, and she pulled the slip over her head.

After making love, they lay beside each other, face-to-face. Jack absentmindedly ran his fingers through her hair.

"Do you feel how much I love you?" he asked.

"Yes."

"Good. Don't forget."

✦ ✦ ✦

When the alarm rang the next morning, they lay in bed a bit longer to hold each other, then got up to brush their teeth. Jack hopped in the shower, and Tess returned to the bedroom. When Jack came out, Tess was balled up in a chair in the corner of the room.

He knelt in front of her. "Sweetheart, what's wrong?"

"It's just . . . I haven't been alone in a week. The last time I was at home by myself . . ."

He pulled her toward him. "It's okay. It's okay. If it's too soon, I can stay with you or you can come with me."

"I need to be able to do this, so please be supportive. It's just a little harder than I thought. You won't be there with me."

"We can FaceTime all day, any time you want to talk or see me, even if it's every five minutes. And if you want me to come home or to pick you up, just say the word. Promise me you will."

"I promise," she said.

"Hang on." Jack got up and went to put on some music. He selected "All of Me" and then walked over to Tess, extending his hand. "Dance with me, my love."

He put his hand on the small of her back, and she leaned against his chest. They swayed to the music, lost in the comfort of their embrace. When the song was over, Jack whispered, "Now you can feel me all day." She smiled and they kissed.

When Jack got into his car, he sat for a long moment to compose himself. He called Tess as soon as he got to his office. She sounded out of breath. "Honey, I'm just finishing my run, can we talk later?"

"Sure," he replied.

An hour and a half later, she FaceTimed him from outside the library.

"Hey, honey. I'm about to go into the library, and I just wanted to say hi."

"How are you doing?"

"Fine, I guess. But I miss your face."

"I miss yours too," he said.

"See you later."

Three hours passed, and Jack hadn't heard from Tess. He was wary of being overbearing, so he texted Omar, who had spoken to her an hour earlier. Jack still found it incredibly difficult not to check on her, and he eventually gave in.

She answered his FaceTime call, seated in the library stacks, her glasses askew. She whispered, "Hey, baby. They don't allow cell phone use. You're going to get me in trouble."

"I just wanted to see your pretty face," he said quietly. She smiled.

"How's it going?" he asked.

"I just read the most fascinating study about how our brains process literature. I'll tell you about it tonight, but for now, I really need to go. I have a lot to get through, and the reference librarian is giving me dirty looks."

"Okay, sweetheart. I'll see you tonight. How about I pick up takeout?"

"Sounds great. Love you."

"I love you too," he said.

Jack felt a wave of relief. He was grinning from ear to ear when Joe knocked on his door.

"You look like you just got some good news," Joe said.

"I just FaceTimed with Tess. She's doing research for her book. She seemed good. Really good, actually. Like her old self."

Jack noticed Tess seemed more at ease with each passing day. Initially, he saw signs that she was still working through something internally, like when he observed her methodically moving her food around her plate. But the lighter moments returned, such as the evening they were lying on the couch watching an old movie and sharing a tub of popcorn. Tess was jokingly hogging the popcorn, and when Jack tried to take it from her, she threw a few kernels at him. "You did *not* just do that," he said, tossing a handful at her and then tickling her mercilessly until they were both laughing so hard they had to catch their breath. Before long, Tess was immersed in her book project, Jack was back to feeling fully invested at work, they saw their friends every Friday night, and each day they laughed and loved more. They were happy. But then, on the Wednesday exactly six weeks from the day Jack found Tess hiding in the closet, something changed.

Chapter 16

Wednesday morning when the alarm sounded, Tess hopped out of bed before Jack could even say good morning. Knowing her as intimately as he did, he was immediately concerned.

When she emerged from the bathroom, he walked over and slung his arms around her waist. "You got out of bed so quickly I couldn't even kiss you good morning."

"Just trying to get a jump start on the day," she said, slipping out from his arms. "I'll go make coffee."

When Jack was dressed and came into the kitchen, he saw Tess struggling to sort almonds. He watched as she spilled some out on the counter, started counting them, and then pushed them all back together and started again. He approached her from behind and put his hand on her shoulder.

"What are you doing, love?"

"I'm trying to make my snack. You know that Omar makes me bring a snack everywhere, but I keep messing up," she said, her hands trembling.

He placed his hand over hers. "That's okay. I'll do it for you."

"Twelve almonds in each Ziploc. No broken ones, please," she instructed, stepping to the side.

He prepared the bags and placed the lid on the tub of almonds. "Here you go," he said.

"Thank you."

"Sweetheart, what's wrong?" he asked gently.

"I'm just having a stressful workweek."

"Do you promise that's all it is?"

"Yes," she replied.

"I can stay home today if you want. We can hang out."

"Jack, please go to work. I'm fine. I'm gonna jump in the shower."

She tried to sneak past him, but he took her hand and said, "Hey. Just wait a second, please." He leaned in and kissed her tenderly. "I love you."

"Love you too," she said before walking off.

As soon as he heard the shower turn on, he called Omar and said, "Hey, Omar, it's Jack. Something's up with Tess. She was squirrelly this morning when we got up, and then she was shaky and counting her food. She hasn't done that in ages. She said she's just having a stressful workweek, but I'm worried."

"She's okay."

"Then you know what's going on with her?"

"She didn't confide in me, but yes, I know what's troubling her. It's nothing like what you're thinking. It truly is work related, and for a normal person it wouldn't be anything bad, quite the contrary. I don't like keeping things from you when you're concerned, but I want to give her the chance to tell you herself."

"Are you sure she's okay?" Jack asked.

"Yes, as much as Tess ever is. We have our usual breakfast tomorrow; I'll try to talk to her."

"Thank you," Jack said.

"I promise that if she doesn't tell you what's going on by Friday night, I'll tell you when we come over for game night."

"Okay. Bye."

"Bye."

Jack called to check on Tess several times that day and promised to pick up her favorite Indian takeout on the way home. He came home early with the food and a bouquet of white hydrangeas.

"Thank you, baby. They're beautiful," she said.

They sat on the couch eating dinner and watching an old movie. When they went to bed, Jack snuggled up behind her and draped his arm over her. They woke up the next morning exactly as they had fallen asleep.

Tess leapt out of bed and went to brush her teeth. When she exited the bathroom, Jack was standing there. He gave her hand a squeeze and said, "Wait for me."

He disappeared into the bathroom and when he emerged, he approached Tess and caressed the sides of her body. "I'm enforcing the house code."

She smiled. He began kissing her, moving from her mouth to her neck to her ear. He picked her up and carried her to the bed. After making love, they lay gazing at each other. "I love you with my whole heart, forever," he said, staring at her with total adoration.

"I love you too. You're going to be late. You should get going."

"Okay, baby."

At noon, he called Omar to ask about breakfast with Tess.

"She sent me a text message to cancel," Omar said.

"I'm really worried."

"I promise you she's okay. I know exactly what this is about. I'm still hoping she'll tell you herself, but if not, I'll tell you tomorrow night."

Jack reluctantly agreed.

The next morning, Tess tried to leap out of bed, but Jack stopped her. "Hey, please just stay here with me for a minute."

She lay back down.

He ran his finger along her hairline. "Can I ask you something?"

"Uh-huh."

"When you wake up each morning, have you ever thought to yourself, *Today I can die*, or *Today I can live*?"

"No. I just get up and go on with the day."

He cuddled her and said, "Okay."

"I do think about how grateful I am that you're here."

He smiled. "I know you try to be in the moment, it's just . . ."

"What?" she asked. "You can tell me."

He swept his fingers along her cheek. "At our wedding, when Abdul told us that story about the mob, you said you weren't afraid because you didn't care what happened to you."

"Yes, that's true," she said softly.

"That terrifies me," he replied.

She leaned her forehead against his for an intimate moment, drew back, looked deeply into his eyes, and said, "I never wanted to die, but there were times when maybe I didn't want to live." He inhaled sharply. She stroked his cheek and continued, "That hasn't been true for a long time. Jack, I do want to live, with you. Forever and always."

"Me too," he whispered.

"Now let's get on with the day."

He chuckled "Okay, love."

She slipped out of bed and headed to their bathroom.

Later, Jack again found Tess in the kitchen struggling to sort almonds. Without a word, he gently took over the task.

"Thank you," she said. She looked up at him like she was about to cry.

"What is it, baby? Can't you tell me what's going on?" he asked.

"It's just a bad workweek. There's no reason to dwell on it. I'll be fine once this week is over. I promise."

"Everyone's supposed to come here for game night, but I can cancel if you want."

"No, don't do that. It'll be nice to hang out with the gang, and I already bought tons of food."

"Okay," he said.

"Jack, I really am fine. I promise."

He went to work, but he thought about Tess all day. They spoke once at lunchtime, but when he called later in the day, she didn't answer and her voicemail was full.

Chapter 17

When Jack got home, Tess was arranging a crudités platter in the kitchen. He noticed two bouquets of flowers at the end of the bar.

"Those are pretty," he remarked. "Who are they from?"

"My publisher."

"I tried calling you a few times. Did you know that your voicemail is full?"

"Sorry, I turned my ringer off."

"Hey, don't I get a kiss?" he asked.

"I'm sorry, baby. I'm just trying to get everything ready before they get here," she replied. She walked over and gave him a quick kiss.

"Joe went on a second date with that artist you set him up with. He's crazy about her, says he owes you big time," Jack said.

Tess smiled. Just then, the timer beeped. "The quiche is ready," she said.

"It smells good. I'm going to go change and then I'll help."

"Great."

As Jack was walking past the flowers, he noticed a card. Tess was preoccupied with the food, so he glanced at it. The card read: *Sometimes good things happen to good people. I'm so happy for you that I could pop. Love, Claire.*

Everyone was standing around the kitchen making small talk as Tess placed the cheese and charcuterie platter on the bar.

"Where are Omar and Clay?" Joe asked.

"I guess they're running late," Tess replied. "Maybe they got held up at work."

"The traffic was bad," Bobby said, taking a swig of his beer.

The doorbell rang. Jack hit the buzzer and opened the door for Omar and Clay, whose hands were full.

"Sorry we're late," Omar said, flitting inside, holding a jumbo pink cardboard cake box. Clay followed behind with a brown paper bag under one arm and a vase of white flowers in the other. "We had to stop to pick up celebratory supplies," Omar explained, kissing Tess on the forehead and placing the large pastry box on the counter. "We have the most wonderful cake."

"And I have lots of champagne, and of course, a bottle of the best sparkling water for you, Tess," Clay added. "These are for you," he said, handing Tess the flowers.

Tess smiled sheepishly and placed them on the bar in front of her. She looked at Omar. "Who told you?"

"Crystal," he replied, taking off his coat and handing it to Clay.

"She's fired," Tess said.

"No, she's not," Omar said. "Besides, the press release went out yesterday. The whole literary world knows, Butterfly."

"There was a press release?" Tess groaned.

Omar rolled his eyes. "Of course. You know how these things work."

Tess was silent as everyone in the room stared at her.

Omar looked around. "Hmm, two bouquets. I know of at least thirty people who asked for your address. I'm guessing you had deliveries all day."

Tess looked down. "I had them picked up and taken to a local hospital. Those came after the pickup."

"Uh-huh, hiding the evidence, I see," Omar said. "Not the sign of well-being."

"Oh, hush," Tess said.

Jack looked at Tess and Omar. "What are we celebrating?"

"Oh, sweet Butterfly, you haven't even told Jack? Just when I thought you were getting close to sanity," Omar said, kissing her forehead again.

"Perish the thought," Tess whispered. She looked up, everyone's eyes on her. She focused on Jack. "It's nothing," she insisted. "There's no reason to make a fuss. It's not a big deal."

"If by 'not a big deal,' you mean 'a hugely big deal,' then you'd be right," Omar countered. "You see, our very own brilliant Tess has won the highly coveted American Novel Award for her last book."

Jack grinned from ear to ear. "That's so great!"

"Wow, congratulations!" Joe exclaimed.

Everyone chimed in with congratulatory words.

"That's not all," Omar said. "For mere mortals, this would be an incredible achievement, but Tess is anything but ordinary. It's a historic win."

"The word 'historic' is really overused," Tess protested. "Just because something hasn't happened before doesn't mean it's historic."

"Uh, actually, that's literally what it means," Omar countered.

"I have to side with him on that one," Bobby said.

Tess rolled her eyes.

"Tess has won this award before," Omar explained. "She's the first author to ever win twice. And she was the youngest recipient, so actually, she's made history twice."

Tess gave him the side-eye.

Jack was beaming. "That's amazing," he gushed, wrapping her in a hug.

"Wow, Tess. That's truly an incredible achievement," Joe said.

"We're so happy for you," Bobby added.

Tess looked down, seemingly embarrassed by the attention. She smiled half-heartedly and mumbled, "Thanks. I'll go get the cake plates from the china cabinet." She headed toward the dining room.

Joe furrowed his brow. "What's going on?"

Everyone leaned in. Omar quietly said, "We are going to celebrate this. It must be celebrated. When she comes back, please go sit down in the living room and talk about her writing and books. She likes talking about those things. Just don't mention the award. Jack, stay behind with me for a minute."

Tess shuffled back in and held her hands up to show the cake plates. "I'll put these in there," she said quietly, heading into the living room. "Jack, can you bring some forks, please?"

"Sure, sweetheart."

"Jack and I will pour the bubbly. Be there in a flash," Omar added.

Everyone followed Tess into the living room, except for Jack and Omar.

Jack waved Omar to the far side of the kitchen and quietly said, "Listen, I appreciate what you're trying to do, but she's been off for days."

"That's because she has no ability to embrace her

success. I've been watching this same cycle for over fifteen years. It ends tonight. This is a massive achievement, and she deserves to enjoy it."

"I know how much you care about her, but she's been happy until this week. I can't forget that it was only six weeks ago that . . . that I was afraid of losing her. Do you remember how fragile and dissociated she was? I don't think we should push her."

"Jack, I know how protective you are. I would lay down my own life before I would hurt her. I believe we can help her. I know we can. I need you to trust me. Please."

Jack inhaled deeply.

"She deserves every happiness in this life," Omar said.

"What do you need me to do?" Jack asked.

"Just be there with her, supportively. She feels the most comfortable with you around. I'll take care of everything else."

Jack nodded. "Promise you'll shut it down if it's too much."

"Of course," Omar agreed. "And Jack, if I'm able to get her there, whatever you say or do, no matter how small, it will matter more than anything else. That's what she'll remember."

"Where are you guys?" Tess called.

"Just getting the drinks, sweetheart," Jack replied.

Tess sat on the far side of the couch. Jack sat beside her with Bobby to his left. Joe, Gina, and Clay were seated in chairs around the coffee table. After handing everyone their champagne flutes, Omar sat in the recliner adjacent to Tess.

"So, let's have a toast," Omar proposed, raising his glass.

Tess raised her glass. "To friendship," she said, before anyone else had a chance to speak.

"Oh, Butterfly," Omar grumbled, shaking his head. "To friendship."

"To friendship," everyone echoed.

Tess took a sip of her sparkling water and set her glass on the coffee table.

Joe said, "Tess, you never finished what you were going to say." He turned to Jack and Omar. "Tess was just about to tell us if she has a favorite line from any of her books."

"Over the years, I felt like I revealed so much of myself in my novels, so the one thing I kept private is what they each mean to me. I felt like it was the only thing I had left that was mine. The things that mean the most to me are quotidian; they are nothing that would stand out to anyone else. There are a few lines that readers constantly bring up, but I never share my favorite. But I'll tell you."

"You know anything you tell us stays in this room," Bobby assured her.

"Absolutely," Joe added.

"I bet I know," Omar said. "They are your favorite words, after all."

Tess smiled. "Yeah."

Omar continued. "The female character says, 'Do you remember?' and the male character says, 'I remember.' It's so simple, but I know that's your favorite bit."

Tess nodded. "It's hard to explain. I guess I think there's nothing more affirming than a shared memory. To me, it's like someone saying, 'You exist and I see you.' That's all people really want."

"Ooh, that's from *Blue Moon*," Gina said. "That's my favorite book. I love it so much. I did notice that part. Hearing what it means to you makes me realize that I was right to think those were special words."

Tess smiled.

Omar leaned forward in his chair. "Tess, we so badly want to celebrate this achievement with you."

She sighed.

"I know you think awards are ridiculous," Omar said.

"Because they are," she quipped back.

"And I know you think humility is a virtue," he added.

"Because it is," she replied.

"But I've never believed those are the reasons you can't seem to find any happiness in your success. I know you think I'm torturing you," Omar continued.

"Because you are," she replied.

"Just tell us why. I've watched for so many years, and it's like every kind word or bit of recognition hurts you, like it physically hurts you. Please tell us why."

"The people's high priestess of pain is crowned again. I just want the coronation to end."

"Oh, Butterfly."

"Okay, I'll tell you," she said softly, curling her legs up on the couch. "When my first novel came out, I was inundated with emails and letters from readers telling me how they connected to the book. They would tell me their stories—all kinds of horrible traumas, abuse, self-hatred, self-harm, depression, all manner of suffering. At book signings, people would wait in line for hours just to whisper their stories to me. It's been like that ever since with each book. You see, books do well when they resonate. The success of my books reflects only one thing: how many people are in pain. I just don't know how to celebrate that."

"Is that really how you see it?" Omar asked.

"Yes," Tess whispered.

"Oh, sweet Butterfly, don't you understand what 'inspirational' means? That's what they call your novels."

"Tess," Gina said. "You know I'm a huge fan of your work, but I never told you this when we met because I didn't want to make you uncomfortable. For years, I was in one toxic relationship after another. The guy I was with before Bobby liked to use me as a punching bag. I read *Candy Floss* for strength. When I finished reading it, I decided to change my life. With the courage I found in your words, I walked out and never looked back. I honestly don't think I'd be here without it. I've read it so many times that the pages are falling out. Yes, it resonated with me because I was in pain, but it also saved me."

"It's true," Bobby said. "She wanted to tell you ages ago."

Tess smiled faintly.

Joe chimed in. "I read *The Island* about five or six years ago. I was going through a tough time. We see so much horror in our line of work. It helped restore my faith in humanity. Truly, it did. There was no rosy version of reality. It was gritty but hopeful. I needed that more than I knew at the time. Pain and suffering are inevitable in this world. Your books don't cause the pain or celebrate it; they offer respite."

"Thanks, guys," Tess muttered. "I appreciate it. I do."

"You know what I think we need? Cake," Omar said, leaping up.

Tess leaned on Jack. He embraced her, rubbing her arm.

"When he ordered this cake, he said it was the happiest he had ever been to buy something in his entire life," Clay said.

"He's very sweet," Tess replied. Then she whispered to Jack, "I don't eat cake."

"We can share a piece," he suggested, dropping a kiss in her hair.

"Shut your eyes, Tess!" Omar hollered.

Tess obliged. When she opened them, there was a large round cake in the center of the table. In gold script, it said, *Congratulations, Tess! We love you!* Dozens of gold and silver shooting stars surrounded the lettering and borders of the cake.

Tess gasped. She leaned forward. Her eyes flooded with hot tears. "It's wonderful. I can't believe you remembered."

"How could I ever forget?" Omar replied.

"That's the only time I ever shared that story with anyone," she said, happy tears streaming down her face.

"I assumed," he replied.

She wiped her cheeks and looked up at the group. "It was years ago. We were in Chicago. I had been on the road for months doing book talks and signings. I was doing a bunch of stops in Illinois, and when I was in Urbana-Champaign, I caught a terrible cold. I was mostly upset because I had been looking forward to meeting Omar in Chicago." She turned to Jack. "Remember, we told you about that night."

He nodded.

"Anyway, we hadn't seen each other in months and we were meant to have fun together, but by then I was too sick. So, he stayed with me in my hotel suite. We ordered loads of room service and watched *Moulin Rouge* for the billionth time. I was on so much cold medicine, and I was hugely grumpy."

"She was," Omar interjected with a smile. "God, she's an awful patient."

Tess giggled. "So, to try to cheer me up, he acted out each dance number."

"Smashingly, I might add," Omar said, batting his eyelashes for dramatic effect.

Tess smiled. "You were marvelous, such flair. And it did cheer me up. After the movie ended and we were done gorging ourselves, we lay in bed talking. There's a scene in the movie where Satine sings a song called, 'Someday I'll Fly Away.' It's the most subtle number in the film, but it was so powerful. She sings about how she's dreamt of flying away her whole life, but she wonders if it's worth it to dream because of what might happen when the dreams end." She turned to face Omar. "You've always wanted to know why I love that movie so much; it's that song." She turned back to the group. "I was thinking about that song, and that's when I told him." She stopped to take a breath. "You all know what my childhood was like."

They nodded.

"I didn't believe in God, so I didn't have anything to pray to for help. One day, my aunt gave me a packet of those glow-in-the-dark shooting star stickers. She said if you make a wish on a shooting star, it comes true. So I stuck the stickers on the ceiling above my bed, and every night I wished on them over and over and over again. I stared at the shooting stars above. No matter how tired I was, I forced myself to stay awake as long as I possibly could to keep wishing. I always wished for the same thing. I made that wish for years," she said, wiping a tear from her eye.

Jack rubbed her arm.

"Eventually, I stopped believing. The day I moved out of that horrible house, I had two clear thoughts: I wanted to write so that I could give people something to believe in, even if I didn't; and I never wanted to see another shooting star again. I couldn't bear to live in a world where you can wish thousands of times and your wish never comes true."

"I thought it was safe now," Omar said. "You never said what your single wish was, but I believe I know. And I believe it has come true."

"It has," she whispered.

"What was your wish?" Jack asked softly.

She looked at him. "This. I wished for exactly what I have, with all of you," she said, looking at the faces of her beloved friends, "and especially you," she added, turning to Jack and squeezing his hand.

"Tess," Omar said.

She turned to face him.

"You have spent your entire adult life turning darkness into light. In doing so, you've helped countless people, including the ones in this room. That is why your readers love you, and that is why you've received recognition for your work. That is what this award honors: transforming darkness into light. And *that* is something that ought to be celebrated."

She sniffled, took a breath, and said, "Okay. I can celebrate that."

Omar smiled. "Come here," he said, rising.

She stood up and hugged him tightly. "Thank you."

"I'm so happy for you. You're brilliant and you deserve this."

"Thank you," she whispered again.

"And you will always have two men who love you beyond measure," he said.

When they separated, she wiped her face and said, "Well, I guess someone should cut the cake."

"That's my job," Clay said, picking up the knife.

As he was passing out pieces of cake, Tess sat down and leaned against Jack.

"I'm so proud of you," he whispered.

She smiled.

"Are you two sharing?" Clay asked, his arm outstretched with a plate.

"I'll have my own," Tess said. "Just a small piece, please."

"Now that we've had dessert, everyone help yourselves to some food," Tess said, gesturing toward the kitchen. "Are you coming?" she asked Jack as she started to get up.

"I'll be right there. Omar and I will clean up the cake plates."

Clay carried the leftover cake, and everyone headed into the kitchen. Jack looked at Omar. "Thank you for what you did for Tess. She's lucky to have you. I couldn't have done that."

Omar smiled. "It wouldn't have been possible without you. Any happiness she has now is because of you."

"The happiness I have is because of her."

"You two were made for each other." He let out a puff. "I've loved Tess from the moment we met. I've always seen who she is, who she's meant to be. I've been ridiculously proud witnessing all she's accomplished. Yet it's also been hard knowing she hasn't been able to enjoy it. I don't have the words to tell you how happy I am to see her finally able to enjoy her extraordinary life, because of the ordinary love she craved."

Jack smiled. "I'm grateful that she has two men who will always love her so fiercely." He put his arm on Omar's shoulder, leaned in to hug him, and said, "We're family."

"Forever," Omar agreed.

They collected the plates and joined the others. Tess was serving Gina a slice of quiche when the doorbell rang.

"I'll get it," Jack said. He returned a moment later with a vase of long-stemmed red roses. "Sweetheart, you got a flower delivery."

She smiled. "That's nice. They're gorgeous."

Jack looked at the card and did a double take. "Uh, do you have a friend named Bruce?"

"I have two friends named Bruce," she replied. "Gina, you would love this guy I know; he's an elementary school art teacher, and he does the most amazing puppet-making project with his kids."

"Sweetheart, is your other friend a musician, by chance?" Jack asked.

"Yup," she said, serving Joe some quiche.

"I think this is from him," Jack said, placing the vase on the counter. "Do you want to see the card?"

"Can you read it?" she asked.

"Blinded by the light always. Well done. Love, Bruce."

"Oh, that's sweet," Tess said.

Bobby's jaw dropped. "You know Jack loves his music."

"Oh, well you should meet him sometime. Great guy. Bobby, would you like some quiche?"

Bobby stared at Jack wide-eyed before looking at Tess and mumbling, "Uh, yes, please. Thank you."

They filled their plates and returned to the living room.

After tasting the eggplant dip, Omar said, "Butterfly, this is delicious. Is it Layla's recipe? You know how I love it."

Tess nodded and jumped up. "I should probably give Bruce a quick call to thank him for the flowers."

As soon as she left the room, Gina asked, "Why do you call her Butterfly?"

Jack looked up from his plate. "I asked her once after we first met, but she said she didn't know. I've always wondered."

Omar laughed. "I've been calling her that since her first book came out. She never asked why. She just accepted it."

"Is it because butterflies are so beautiful?" Gina asked.

"Metamorphosis?" Joe asked.

Jack shook his head. "I think it's the butterfly effect."

Omar smiled. "Yes, you're on to it. The butterfly effect essentially says that something as small as a butterfly flapping her wings can change the entire world. I've always found it to contain a paradox: tragedy and beauty. The butterfly will never understand how the flap of her wings has changed the world, and therein is her tragedy. But because she can never understand her impact, she has only the moment, the very movement of her wings, and so she is always fully present in the now. And therein is her beauty."

Jack smiled.

Tess returned and plopped back down on the couch.

"How's Bruce?" Omar asked.

"Good. He's writing a new song. The lyrics are wonderful. So you all co-opted this evening, but it's still a game night. What are we playing?"

"That's my Butterfly," Omar said.

Tess and Jack were nestled together on the couch. "No one wanted to play Jenga with you since you've defused bombs and all, but after your colossal loss, I'm a little concerned that the country isn't as safe as I thought," Tess teased.

"You distracted me," Jack protested.

"I did nothing of the sort. I feel a little guilty we're not helping clean up. You guys are spoiling us!" she called out to their friends.

"You can't do the dishes at your own celebration," Omar replied.

"We'll have this place spotless in no time," Joe said.

"Make sure you all take some of the leftover food and cake!" Tess hollered.

"I'm on it," Clay called.

Jack ran his fingers through Tess's hair. "We have the best friends," she said.

"Yeah, we do," he agreed. "You know, Omar finally told us why he calls you Butterfly. Do you want to know?"

"Not really."

He chuckled. "He would have guessed as much." He squeezed her hand. "I'm so proud of you. Have I told you that?"

"Uh-huh."

"It's a big weekend. What should we do to celebrate?" he asked.

"Normal stuff. Let's go to a movie, or watch a game, or take a walk. I just want to be together."

He pulled her chin to him and gently pressed his lips to hers. "Okay."

She nuzzled into him and looked up at the mantel covered in framed photos of the two of them, her and Omar, Gracie, and all their friends. "Jack, do you remember the first night we met when I said that reality never lives up to our dreams?"

"I remember."

"Perhaps it's our dreams that can never capture all that is actually possible."

Epilogue

Four Months Later

"We're deeply honored to have you back at New York University, Ms. Lee. There's been so much excitement for your visit that you'll see the auditorium is completely packed, standing room only."

Tess smiled, holding Jack's hand as their host guided them backstage. They passed a custodian who glanced at Tess and looked down as if starstruck. She walked over and shook his hand. Once they reached the backstage wing, her host said, "There's water on stage for you. Are you sure I can't get you anything else?"

"I'm fine, thank you."

"After I introduce you, I thought we could spend half an hour having a conversation, and then open it up for audience questions for the last fifteen minutes before the book signing."

"Sure," Tess replied.

"How long would you like to stay at the signing?" he asked.

"Until everyone's had their books signed," she replied. Jack chuckled.

"Wonderful," her host replied. "A few of us were planning to take you to The Odeon in Tribeca afterward for lunch. I remembered you liked it there."

"Perfect. Thank you."

"Well, this is it," he announced. "I'm going to introduce you."

He walked onstage and Tess stayed with Jack.

"Welcome to this very special event. There's so much I could say about Tess Lee. I would love to list her books, her awards, and share some of the things that have been written about her over the years, but she asked me not to do any of that."

The audience laughed.

"I suppose it doesn't matter; you're all gathered here because you already know those things. Instead, I will just share what today means to me. Tess Lee's books have brought me comfort, hope, and strength. On dark days, they have been the words in my head, reminding me that there is light at the end of the tunnel. When Ms. Lee accepted the invitation to speak here today, I was overcome. Then she called me herself to tell me how much she was looking forward to it. Yeah, I did a happy dance in my office. So, it is my great honor to introduce author Tess Lee."

Jack kissed Tess. "Knock 'em dead, Mrs. Miller."

Tess walked onstage to a standing ovation.

After their conversation about the power of literature, the host invited questions from the audience. The Q&A went smoothly and quickly, and before long, there was only time for one final question. A woman stood up and said, "Your characters are always fighting personal battles, many related to past traumas, but your books have hopeful messages. Do you believe that healing is possible?"

"I don't think I'm any better equipped to answer that than anyone else in this room, but I will share this from my own experience. When I was in high school, I had a boyfriend who wanted to get married. I didn't feel that way about him and ended the relationship. He told me, 'No one will ever be able to fill the hole in your soul.' I still remember those words like it happened yesterday. He was hurt, and he wanted to hurt me in return. For a long time, those words haunted me like a shadow. Eventually, I realized that we're lucky if we end up with a hole in our soul. You see, our wounds don't start out that way. They're jagged. They have rough edges. They are like flesh that has been ripped from our body. If we learn to let love into our lives, over time, the jagged edges become smooth, and only a hole remains. Sometimes that love comes from a friend's laughter, the hug of a child, or the embrace of a lover who sees who we really are. Sometimes giving love freely and with your whole heart can heal you too. When there aren't people to provide that love, it can come from a song, or a movie, or even a novel. And that is why I write."

Read on for a special preview of the second Celestial Bodies Romance, *Twinkle of Doubt*, in which Tess, Jack, and their chosen family explore the nature of doubt and the struggle to feel worthy of love. Look for *Twinkle of Doubt* in spring 2026.

Twinkle of Doubt

Chapter 1

"Thank you, I've got it from here," Jack said to the driver, taking the luggage and seeing him out. He turned to Tess. "Welcome home, Mrs. Miller."

She smiled, removed the lei from around her neck, and placed it on the counter.

"You looked so beautiful running around in the sun. I'm going to miss the leis and the flowers in your hair," Jack said.

"Me too. That was the most incredible vacation I've ever had. Pure paradise. Thank you for making it so special," she replied.

"I still can't believe we never took a honeymoon. What were we thinking? I'm glad we could make up for it for our second anniversary."

"Maui is so beautiful. That house was magical. If we were there right now, we'd probably be relaxing on our private beach or splashing around in the ocean," she said.

"Or making love on the beach. Or on a chaise lounge. Or in the pool. Or in the outdoor shower. Or in every room of the house," Jack said, slipping his hands around her waist. "The way you smelled, the salt water, the coconut oil, the flowers—I'll never forget it. And the taste of pineapple dripping from your lips . . ." He leaned in and kissed her.

"I never thought it was possible to make love so many times in a day. Somehow, even after two years, you still make each time feel like the first," Tess said.

"That's because I fall in love with you all over again every day, every time I look into your big brown eyes. I really do."

She blushed.

"I still can't believe the staff caught us by the pool," Jack said, laughing.

Tess giggled. "Well, it was very chivalrous of you to try to cover me up with that towel."

"We should have stayed longer. Ten days wasn't enough. Getting a break from work only highlighted how stressful it is to think about terrorism day in and day out. After years of seeing the worst in humanity, I started to forget that some people live differently."

"I know. You needed a Technicolor break; you've been on the dark side for too long. But I thought it would be nice to spend our actual anniversary in our own home, the same place we got married. Plus, I didn't think you should use up all your vacation time," she said.

"Baby, I'd quit my job and move to Maui if you wanted. I'm serious. We could buy that house."

"You'd miss your work."

He shrugged. "I'd get over it."

"And our friends," she said.

"They'd visit."

She looked down. "I don't think I could survive without Omar. It's been him and me since our first day of college."

He put his hand on her face, she looked into his sea-blue eyes, and he pulled her close in a comforting embrace. "I know what his friendship means to you. I'm just saying that you can write from anywhere, so if you ever decide that you want to pack up and be a beach bum with me, I'd be all in. And I'm pretty sure that Omar and Clay would make good use of the guesthouse."

"Maybe if you let me drive the motorcycle or pilot the helicopter next time, I'll consider it," she said.

He laughed. "The idea is to *live*. I think you need a few lessons first, sweetheart. Plus, I loved feeling your arms wrapped around me when we took those sharp bends around the cliffs."

"That was so much fun. I'd never been on a Harley before. You made me feel safe and so free."

"That's exactly how I want you to feel, always, just like I promised you on the day we got married, standing right over there."

"Jack, I love you so much. Happy anniversary."

"I love you with my whole heart, forever. Happy anniversary, sweetheart. Let's go to bed. I'm not done with you yet."

When Jack's alarm rang the next morning, he tried to sneak out of bed quietly.

"Hey you, get back here," Tess said.

"Go back to sleep," he whispered.

"I can't," she said, sitting up and stretching her arms. "Omar's coming over for breakfast. We have a lot to catch up on."

"I'm still shocked that you didn't bring your phone to Hawaii. I didn't think you could go that long without texting him."

"He understood. I didn't want anything to interrupt our romantic getaway. Besides, he knew how to get a hold of us if there was an emergency."

"I'm going to hop in the shower," Jack said. "I can only imagine what's waiting for me at the office."

"Okay, baby. I'll make coffee."

"Thank you," he said, leaning down for a quick smooch.

Half an hour later, Tess handed Jack a tumbler of coffee. "Have a great day, baby."

"You know I always miss you when we're not together, but it'll be even worse than usual today," he said.

She smiled. "For me too."

"Tell Omar I said hello," he told her on his way out the door.

✦ ✦ ✦

"Aloha, Butterfly," Omar said, placing a bag and a manila folder on the counter before squeezing her tightly.

"Oh, I missed you and your gorgeous English accent so much," Tess replied.

"I brought bagels. I'm hoping you're so blissed out from your tropical sex romp that you're willing to eat a few empty carbs. There's a fruit salad too, in case I overshot."

She giggled. "I've been really good about my eating, actually. You'd be proud of me. I can't remember the last time I counted my food or purposely skipped a meal. I just feel so content in my own skin now, because of Jack. I don't need to do that anymore, at least not all the time."

Omar smiled. "I'm so happy you're embracing the love you deserve."

She squeezed his hand and said, "I'm trying."

"Okay, so carbs it is. I also brought along a few work things, if you're in the mood. I've been running your publishing empire flawlessly as usual, but I do need to check in with you on a few matters. Come on. You pour the coffee, I'll fix the bagels, and then I want to hear everything. Well, maybe not everything. I do need to be able to look Jack in the eye again."

Soon, they plopped onto the couch and began gabbing. Tess ate half a bagel and gushed about her trip. "The house was marvelous, all one floor, with walls of windows overlooking the ocean. It was remote, up on a cliff. There was a pool and Jacuzzi, a cliffside dining table under a canopy where the staff served our meals, and a heavenly private beach."

"Sounds perfect," Omar said. "Next time, bring me."

"Well, there was a fully equipped guesthouse."

"Now we're talking," he said.

"We went up in a helicopter, and the view took my breath away. The island is gorgeous, all the bright colors: blues, greens, pinks, and purples. You should have seen Jack piloting. He was in his element; it was super sexy."

"I know how you love a man working a big machine," he said with a laugh.

"You're terrible," she replied, playfully hitting his chest. "Jack rented a Harley, too, and drove us all around the island."

"You've always been a bit of a daredevil, my little fearless one, but never thought I'd see the day you rode on a motorcycle. Bloody hell, Butterfly, please tell me you wore a helmet."

"Yes, Jack made me. It was exhilarating. It pushes all the thoughts and worries out of your mind, and you just feel the air, boundless amounts of air."

Omar smiled.

"The best part was being alone together. Every afternoon, Jack would lie down on a chaise lounge by the pool or on the beach, and I'd sit between his legs and lean back against his chest. He'd wrap his arms around me and we'd watch the ocean for hours, waiting for the sky to turn shades of pink and coral. It was the most serene feeling, just being together, in silence, and feeling that close. I didn't know it could ever be like that between two people, and that's how I always feel with him, like we understand each other entirely."

"I honestly can't believe you came back. It sounds like nirvana; you should've stayed," Omar said.

"Actually, Jack wants to quit his job so we could go live there."

"Jack's a smart man."

Tess raised her eyebrows in disbelief.

"Well, Butterfly, why the hell not? You're barely forty years old and you have over five hundred million dollars, not to mention a private jet you barely use anymore. You have the means and ability to live any life you choose. You can write from anywhere."

"But Jack's job is here in DC," she said.

"Jack's been serving his country since he was eighteen years old. That's over twenty-five years. He's served with dedication and honor. He can retire young and enjoy himself. If he wants to work, I'm sure there's a wealth of consulting or specialty work he could do with his experience. Perhaps he could do volunteer work."

"Our friends are here. You're here," she said.

"Butterfly, if you buy an estate in Hawaii, I promise to wear out my welcome in your guest quarters. We've lived in separate cities before, and we always spent more time together than apart. Besides, you don't have to do it full-time. You could buy something there and keep this place for vacations or split your time between the two. You still have the house in Los Angeles in between. Why not get some use out of it? Hell, you could buy homes anywhere you choose.

I know you'd love to have an apartment in New York or Tokyo. There's no need to be stuck here all the time. Jack hardly needs to keep doing the daily grind, nor do you. Why not live exactly the life you want? You both deserve to just be happy together. Most people only dream of that kind of freedom. You have the ability to turn your dream into reality. What's stopping you?"

She looked down.

"Let's do a little exercise. Without censoring yourself, tell me the things about your life, personal and professional, past and present, that you love."

"Spending time with Jack, with you, and with our friends. Writing, of course. I even liked the book tours, if only they had been shorter and more manageable. I liked traveling to different countries, although I've done enough of that for several lifetimes, so I'm not desperate for it. But all the rest of it—the media and road dog life with events nearly every day—it was exhausting and became too much. You know that. The privacy I have now, I would never want to give up again. A quieter life suits me. Fame never has."

"Butterfly, you could have a life entirely structured around everything you just said. You and Jack can live anywhere, spend all your time together. You could travel where and when you like. Your friends aren't going anywhere, and you know you can't get rid of me. Why not go for it? It sounds like Jack is keen on it."

"It's just . . . well, it's just . . ."

Omar took her hand. "I know what you're really scared of way down deep, but you needn't be. Jack loves you as much as any man has ever loved anyone. He's not going anywhere. I remember his wedding vows, the commitment he made, and Butterfly, he meant every word."

She smiled, her eyes watery.

"Just promise me you'll think about it. You and Jack can have every happiness, any way you both choose. You deserve that. And you can still write your stunningly inspirational novels and do book events wherever and whenever you like. Jack would always be free to travel with you. Hell, he can be your personal security. Few authors have a former federal agent as their bodyguard. It would be very cool. Besides, it would help me sleep at night to know he's there."

She nodded faintly. "Enough about me. How have you been? What have I missed?"

Omar's expression turned sour.

"Oh no. I recognize that look. What's wrong?" she asked, rubbing his hand.

"Things aren't exactly fabulous with Clay right now."

"What's going on?"

"I met him for lunch at the hospital last week and noticed something between him and some guy he works with. I can't explain it, but there was something going on."

"Did you ask him about it?"

"Not right away. I let it fester for a few days until I thought I was going to implode, so then naturally I confronted him in the worst possible way."

"Good job," she joked.

"I know," he said.

"And? What did he say?"

"He said the man had come on to him, but that he turned him down flat. He assured me there's nothing to worry about, nor would there ever be."

"Then why don't you look relieved?"

"Well, he hadn't told me about it. He kept it to himself."

"Maybe he didn't want to upset you over nothing."

"That's exactly what he said."

"Don't you believe him?" Tess asked.

"I want to believe him, and I mostly do. Clay is honest and I trust him. It's just that there's this small kernel of doubt, and when doubt creeps in, it takes up residence like a squatter. You want it out of your mind, but you don't know how to evict it."

"I understand," she said, leaning over and hugging him.

"I know you do," he whispered.

Tess sat back. "I would believe him, though. You two are perfect together," she said. "You've built something solid, and Clay would never jeopardize that. Talk to him about it. Talk to him until you're sure."

"You and Jack have only been together for two years, but you both waited so long for love that I think you just knew what to do with it when it came. Clay and I have been together a lot longer. Sometimes I worry that people stop seeing each other over time; you each become like the wallpaper or a piece of furniture. What if he doesn't see me anymore? That might make something new look quite appealing."

"That's just your doubt speaking. Clay does see you. He doesn't want anyone else. But maybe you need to work on things a bit and not take him for granted. I'm sure every couple goes through this. You both have a million things on your plate, but you have to make sure you can see the trees in the forest. Give more attention to the one thing that matters most; give him your undivided, full attention for a while and see if things improve. That's the decision Jack and I made when we got married. That's what we knew to do with our love: prioritize it. We live that choice every day, and I'm so grateful we do."

"Thank you. You two make it look effortless, but I know it probably isn't. I know nothing grows unless you tend to it."

"Water your garden and it will blossom," she said.

Omar nodded. "I don't care if you tell Jack, but please don't tell anyone else. I don't want people to act strangely around us."

"Of course."

"I could use more fuel. Let's refill our coffee mugs and then go through this," Omar suggested, lifting the manila folder. "It's just a few licensing and foreign translation contracts that require your review and signature."

Tess grabbed the mugs and stood up. "That was another wonderful thing about Maui—I didn't have to be Tess Lee. No one wanted anything from me, and I could just breathe the briny sea air. Even the house staff called me Mrs. Miller. It was bliss. I felt totally like myself."

"Butterfly, you can have that any time you want it. Remember, you and Jack don't owe anyone a thing."

She smiled.

"He loves you, Tess. He's completely and madly in love with you, and he always will be. There's nothing to fear."

"I'll get us that refill, and then you can drag me back into the world of Tess Lee."

Acknowledgments

Thank you to the entire team at She Writes Press, especially Brooke Warner and Shannon Green. I'm incredibly grateful for your unfailing support. I also extend a spirited thank-you to Crystal Patriarche and everyone at BookSparks for helping readers find this book. Thank you to Anne Durette for the stellar copyediting services. Thank you to Katie Lowery at Clear Voice Editing for your work on an earlier version of this book. Thank you to the early reviewers for your generous endorsements. Sincere appreciation to Shalen Lowell, world-class assistant and spiritual bodyguard. Heartfelt thanks to Celine Boyle for your invaluable feedback. Liza Talusan and the Saturday Writing Team—thank you for building such a supportive community and allowing me to be a part of it. To my social media community and colleagues, thank you boundlessly for your support. My deep gratitude to my friends, especially Vanessa Alssid, Melissa Anyiwo, Sandra Faulkner, Ally Field, Jessica Smartt Gullion, Pamela Martin, Laurel Richardson, Xan Nowakowski, Mr. Barry Shuman, Eve Spangler, and

J. E. Sumerau. As always, my love to my family. Madeline Leavy-Rosen, you are my heart. Mark Robins, thank you for all that words cannot capture. To those who walk with us on our healing journeys, I salute you. This book is for everyone, everywhere.

About the Author

Patricia Leavy, PhD, is a best-selling author. She has published over fifty books, earning commercial and critical success in both nonfiction and fiction, and her work has been translated into numerous languages. Over the course of her career, she has also served as series creator and editor for ten book series, and she cofounded *Art/ Research International: A Transdisciplinary Journal*. She has received over one hundred book awards. Recently, *The Location Shoot* won four First-Place Firebird Book Awards. She has also received career awards from the New England Sociological Association, the American Creativity Association, the American Educational Research Association, the International Congress of Qualitative Inquiry, and the National Art Education Association. In 2016, Mogul, a global women's empowerment network, named her an "Influencer." In 2018, the National Women's Hall of Fame honored her, and SUNY New Paltz established the "Patricia Leavy Award for Art and Social Justice." Please visit www.patricialeavy.com for more information.

Author photo © Mark D. Robins

Looking for your next great read?

We can help!

Visit www.shewritespress.com/next-read
or scan the QR code below for a list
of our recommended titles.

She Writes Press is an award-winning
independent publishing company founded to
serve women writers everywhere.